COMING NEXT TIME ...

**STORIES! ARTICLES!
SHERLOCK HOLMES & DR. WATSON!**

Sherlock Holmes Mystery Magazine #28
is just a few months away...watch for it!

Not a subscriber yet?
Send $59.95 for 6 issues (postage paid in the U.S.) to:

**Wildside Press LLC
Attn: Subscription Dept.
7945 MacArthur Blvd, Suite 215
Cabin John, MD 20818**

You can also subscribe online at
www.wildsidepress.com

FROM WATSON'S NOTEBOOKS

Both Holmes and I are pleased to offer "Silver Blaze" in this issue. In this fascinating tale my friend made what is perhaps his most famous remark to Inspector Gregory concerning "the curious incident of the dog in the night-time." (We both also enjoyed Mark Haddon's novel with that title.)

Holmes has mixed feelings, though, about R.J. Lewis's "Death in Baltimore," which to my mind is an arresting inspection of the mysterious death of the American writer Edgar Allan Poe. Two detectives join forces to solve the problem: Holmes's father and Poe's own "first" detective, C. Auguste Dupin. If you have read my earliest ratiocinative adventures, you know—perhaps all too well—that Holmes had a severely negative opinion of Dupin and two of his cases, "The Murders in the Rue Morgue" and "The Mystery of Marie Rogêt," though he admits that he admires the solution, if not the sleuth, of "The Purloined Letter."

We welcome back Hal Charles, whose Kelly Locke stories generously reflect Holmes's mind and character. We regret that these tales have not been seen in *Sherlock Holmes Mystery Magazine* for quite a while. This one is an amusing variation in our "Red-Headed League" adventure; its plot is quite clever and slightly reminded Holmes of the classic Jacques Futrelle puzzle, "The Problem of Cell 13."

The next issue of *Sherlock Holmes Mystery Magazine* will feature "The Adventure of the Beryl Coronet."

And now a few words from my colleague and coeditor Marvin Kaye.

—John H Watson, M D

✗　✗　✗　✗

All of the stories in this, the 27th issue of *Sherlock Holmes Mystery Magazine*, are by authors who have appeared here before, as well as an article by O'Neill Curatolo.

The "recidivists" include in alphabetical order the long-absent ditto missed Hal Charles, Dianne Ell, Ron Goulart—with another risible Harry Challenge adventure, this time one about a purloined "talking horse," with no relationship to TV's Mister Ed or film's Francis the talking mule—R.J. Lewis, whose first of a projected series deals with the death of Edgar Allan Poe, here investigated by Poe's C. Auguste Dupin and the nautically-employed father of Sherlock Holmes! A

SHERLOCK HOLMES
MYSTERY MAGAZINE

VOL. 7, NO. 6   Issue #27

FEATURES

From Watson's Notebooks, *by John H Watson, M D* 4
Ask Mrs Hudson, *by (Mrs) Martha Hudson.* 6

NON FICTION

Screen of the Crime, *by Kim Newman* 11
Carnivory, Darwin, and Doyle, *by O'Neill Curatolo* 15
"Someday the Truth Will Come Out", *by Chris Chan* 18
Dr. Watson and True Facts, *by Bruce Harris* 31

FICTION

The Red-Faced League, *by Hal Charles* 34
Such Good Friends, *by Dianne Neral Ell* 48
The Strange Disappearance of the Talking Horse,
by Ron Goulart. 65
A Death in Baltimore, *by Arjay Lewis* 88
Jewels in the Sun, *by Laird Long.* 109
The Unexpected, *by J.P. Seewald.* 111
"Lease With Option to Buy", *by Ellen Wight* 119

The Adventure of Silver Blaze, *by Sir Arthur Conan Doyle.* 126

ART & CARTOONS

Joe Willey . . . . Front Cover
Marc Bilgrey. 2

Sherlock Holmes Mystery Magazine #27 (Vol. 7, No. 6) is copyright
© 2019 by Wildside Press LLC. All rights reserved.
Visit us online at wildsidepress.com.

STAFF

Publisher: John Betancourt
Editor: Marvin Kaye
Non-fiction Editor: Carla Coupe
Assistant Editor: Steve Coupe

Sherlock Holmes Mystery Magazine is published by Wildside Press, LLC. Single copies: $10.00 + $3.00 postage. U.S. subscriptions: $59.95 (postage paid) for the next 6 issues in the U.S.A., from: Wildside Press LLC, Subscription Dept. 7945 MacArthur Blvd, Suite 215, Cabin John, MD 20818. International subscriptions: see our web site at www.wildsidepress.com. Available as an ebook through all major ebook etailers, or our web site, www.wildsidepress.com.

new story by J.P. Seewald is also included, as is a new short short by Laird Long, and Ellen Wight.

Issue 28 of *Sherlock Holmes Mystery Magazine* will have articles by Gary Lovisi and Janice Law and new fiction (other than Conan Doyle's Beryl Coronet adventure) that includes a new Nero Wolfe mystery and stories by Dan Andriacco, Dana Martin Batory, Marc Bilgrey, Rochelle Campbell, Ellen Denton, Michael Hemmingson, Sharon Hunt, Sanford Zane Meschow.

See you in #28!

Canonically Yours,
Marvin Kaye

ASK MRS HUDSON

by (Mrs) Martha Hudson

It's the time of year I always begin to feel a bit nostalgic. You cannot get where I am in life by dwelling too long upon the past, but there are memories, happy or otherwise, which must always claim one's attention whenever they decide to make an appearance.

So it is, as I sit here in front of my little parlour window with my cup of tea, watching passersby struggle against the sleet. It wasn't sleeting the day I first met Sherlock Holmes. It was, however, cold and rainy, with a few snowflakes mixed in. I know that the world now remembers New Year's Day, 1881, as the day when Sherlock Holmes and John Watson first met in the laboratory at Bart's, but for me, the fateful day was Thursday, the 30th December, 1880. My girl Rosie answered the bell to a tall, thin, rather bedraggled-looking young man clutching the previous day's *Daily Telegraph* in one hand and a tattered umbrella in the other. I took him up to see 221B, mostly because I felt a bit sorry for him; I did not believe for a minute that he would be able to afford the rent, but I did want to get him out of the weather for a bit and perhaps give him some tea. I suppose he inspired maternal feelings in me from the first.

He loved the rooms—particularly the book-cases and the deal table (although why anyone should admire a deal table was beyond me). Over tea and biscuits (ginger nut, I believe), he told me that, while his income was a bit sporadic at the moment, he had a brother in government who could vouch for him and he believed that with a flat-mate, he could manage. When I asked his occupation, he said that he was a "consulting detective." That, in fact, he "invented the job." Well, I have known several private inquiry agents in my time, so I took that last as a young man's bragging. But his enthusiasm and unaffectedness appealed to me. I suppose it sounds strange, seeing as we are discussing a true master of disguise, but when he is with his friends, Sherlock Holmes is as genuine a person as you could ever meet and he was even more so as a young man. It is a rare quality in London, I assure you.

So when he asked—or rather, begged—me to hold the flat for him until he could find someone to share the rent, I agreed—but only for a week, rather than the fortnight he wanted and only if he gave me £1 as deposit. I am a woman of business, after all and to survive in

London, one must put one's head above one's heart. After a moment's hesitation, he agreed and handed over what I later learned was his very last pound. When he told me this, years later, I asked him why he had done so. After all, there were plenty of other flats in the city and I could have very easily taken his money and let the apartment to someone else that evening. He told me that he deduced that I was trustworthy, but I think it more likely that we each decided to take a chance on the other.

I did not hear from my prospective lodger until the morning of the 2nd January, when I was called from wrestling with my household accounts by a banging at the door. My girl Rosie being otherwise occupied, I answered it myself and found Mr Holmes grinning at me, another fellow with him. This man seemed somewhat older, but that might have just been the worn and haggard look about him. Although he was quite brown and his clothes were new, he seemed faded about the edges, as if he were unwell. I soon learned that this was Dr John Watson and that indeed he was not a healthy man, having been wounded at Maiwand and recently ill with typhus. The doctor was pleased with 221B—I do think he was most happy with the notion of living in a space larger than a hotel room. I listened as he and Mr Holmes discussed the terms. With Dr Watson's pension and what he hoped to earn as a physician, along with Mr Holmes's income, they believed they could afford the rent, provided they economised.

Thus I became landlady to the two most famous lodgers in history. Dr Watson was apparently in a rush to get out of his hotel, for he moved in that very evening. I hope he enjoyed that first quiet evening alone, for Heaven knows his life since has not been peaceful! In *A Study in Scarlet*, he wrote that Holmes arrived with "several boxes and portmanteaus," but the fact is, I never thought a young man could have so many possessions! Several of his crates contained equipment and chemicals for his laboratory and there was a trunk of odd clothing that I made him haul up to the lumber-room. Fortunately my home is well-built, for nearly all the rest of it were books. Mr Holmes told me he stored some of his library with his brother, as his landlord in Montague Street thought the floor of that house not sturdy enough for such weight. Even then, my bookshelves were soon loaded up and some of those boxes made their way into the lumber-room as well. I remember noticing the doctor getting a bit tetchy seeing his things rearranged to make way for his new friend's.

Well, of course they were not friends yet and I am not sure that they were until many months later, as each got to know and trust the other. Certainly I spent enough time listening to both of their complaints in those early days. One of them smoked far too much and was untidy; the other was frequently late with his part of their expenses and hosted nightly card games with a group of inebriated friends. I'll leave you to guess which was which.

All went right in the end, though, as I hope it shall for the writer of this issue's query, although I do think she should have made her plans a bit earlier…

✗   ✗   ✗   ✗

Dear Mrs Hudson,

We shall be in London for the Season this year and as it is our first time, I wondered what hotels you would recommend? We imagine that, as you are Sherlock Holmes's landlady, you have a great knowledge of London and that he has learned most of what he knows from you.

Sincerely,
Maude S.

✗   ✗   ✗

Well, Miss S., you are very kind, but I assure you what knowledge Mr Holmes has of London he has gained on his own, on his endless rambles throughout the city, in all sorts of weather—and from his intensive study of maps and plans. I think that there is no-one in the city with a greater knowledge of streets, closes, alleys—and even sewers!

But to tell you the truth, I do not think he thinks much of hotels, unless a crime is committed in one and very little of The Season—except for the number of thefts and confidence schemes which he is called upon to investigate at that time of year. Keep your valuables and your heart locked up tight, Miss S.!

To answer your question, you can, of course, rent an entire furnished house for the Season, but as your family have not already done so, I assume that you are not of the set who can afford several hundred pounds plus expenses. Don't worry, dear—most people can't. If you are frugal and wish to have the true experience of living in London, you might wish to take lodgings, rather than stay in a hotel. Piccadilly is, of course, very fashionable, but it may cost you more than £3 per week; Hanover Street is even more dear. As this is your first Season, you will probably want to save your money for amusements, so I would suggest seeking rooms in Kensington or Bayswater, where you can find comfortable accommodations for £1 1s. or so per week. This amount will cover plain cooking, attendance and linens, although you will need to order your own groceries.

As I live in London and have all my life, I am not well-acquainted with the hotels (other than, of course, their façades, a few tea-rooms and some of their private detectives) so I consulted Charles Pascoe's guide, *London of To-Day: An Illustrated Handbook for the Season*, which you should find at any bookseller in the city. Mr Pascoe fawns over the Hôtel Métropole and it is surely the most stylish hotel in London, but it is too dear for most of us, as are the Langham and the Grand. He suggests the Tavistock in Covent Garden for an old-fashioned English accommodation, or, for the more modern among us, the First Avenue in Holborn—it is not too far from the West End, but just far enough to keep its charges moderate. You do not say anything about your background, my dear, but if you are from a country family, Mr Pascoe says you might prefer Ridler's in Holborn Hill, or the Bedford in Covent Garden—comfortable and suitable for those of us who must economise.

Dr Watson came in a few minutes ago and inquired as to what I was writing. When I said I was giving advice to a young lady about the Season, he asked me to tell you that, while you will doubtless dance and flirt and partake in all of the gayety of London, you must always remember that charming young men are not always to be trusted and if you are hoping to make a match, it is much better to set your sights on a steady young curate at home than a dashing soldier in a ball room. As he was once a dashing soldier himself, I should take him at his word!

Sincerely,

Mrs (Martha) Hudson

⚡   ⚡   ⚡   ⚡

I find that I have prattled on at length for this month's column, but I do have room, I think, for one more question:

Dear Mrs Hudson,

My name is Alfred Higgs and I am twelve years old. I have read all the Sherlock Holmes cases and hope I can be a detective when I grow up. I do not like many foods particularly parsnip or swedes or anything with kidneys. My mother says that she is sure that Sherlock Holmes likes them and that he eats everything you cook and that there is nothing he does not like. Is this true? Is there a food Sherlock Holmes does not like?

Yrs truly

Alfred J.W. Higgs

⚡   ⚡   ⚡

Well, now, Alfred, I expect you should listen to your mother, as she has your best interests at heart and is serving you, I am sure, many healthy and tasty dishes. Sherlock Holmes is a man to emulate in many respects, but I fear that diet is not one of them. He does not take regular meals and even when he does, I am afraid that they are rather light in vegetables and fruits. Both he and Dr Watson prefer meat with potatoes, or eggs and toast and partake of far too many cold suppers. Dr Watson eats everything I serve with alacrity, but there are some dishes for which Mr Holmes has a pronounced dislike. I shall provide the recipe for one of them here because it is, in fact, delicious and your mother might like to try it. Where Mr Holmes got his dislike of oysters I'm sure I don't know...

✗   ✗   ✗   ✗

Oyster Omelet

12 large fresh oysters
½ tsp salt
6 eggs
1 tbsp. sweet cream
pepper and salt to taste

Chop your oysters into small pieces, sprinkle them with the ½ tsp of salt, then allow them to stand in their own liquor for half an hour. Separate the eggs. Beat the yolks into a firm, smooth paste and the whites into a solid froth. Add the cream, salt and pepper to the yolks, then lightly stir in the whites. Melt 1½ oz of butter in a hot frying pan. Once it has completely melted and begins to fry, pour in the egg mixture and quickly add the oysters. Do not stir, but lift with a broad-bladed omelet knife to keep it from burning. Cook for five minutes. To remove the omelet, place a hot dish over the pan with its bottom up, then carefully flip the pan over. Your omelet should slide out nicely. Serve quickly while hot.

And now I must see to my lodgers's tea. Eat what your mother gives you, Master Alfred! There's many in this world who would be glad of a parsnip or two!

✗

SCREEN OF THE CRIME

by Kim Newman

This month, I'm taking a look at a couple of foreign-language Holmesian comedies from the 1930s.

DER MANN, DER SHERLOCK HOLMES WAR (THE MAN WHO WAS SHERLOCK HOLMES) (1937)

Failed Shaftesbury Avenue private eyes Morris Flint (Hans Albers) and Macky McPherson (Heinz Rühmann)—who never seem anything but German—pass themselves off as Sherlock Holmes and Dr. Watson to get free train rides and fine service in a hotel. While pulling off this scam, they get mixed up with innocent orphan heiresses (Marieluise Claudius and Hansi Knoteck as Jane and Mary Berry from Middletown), a ring of crooks run by *femme fatale* Madame Ganymare (Hilde Weissner), and the easily-impressed local police. The case starts with stolen rare postage stamps and leads to the discovery of a forgers' lair under the castle the Misses Berry think they have inherited. Naturally, the mild-mannered swindlers reveal a heroic streak when it comes to helping out nice young ladies. Flint even shows some detective chops (though he doesn't attempt the trademark deductions) as he examines the scene of a (natural) death and picks up on clues which lead to the secret passage.

In the end, our heroes blunder a bit, the forgery ring is apprehended by the police, and the duo are had up for imposture in a very imposing, stuffy courtroom. They cannily argue that they kept saying they were only Flint and Macky (with a wink suggesting these were the fake identities) while suck-up officials insisted they were the famous sleuths. Though we only see them bumbling, it's mentioned that Flint and Macky have broken a lot of other cases during their imposture. They also get the girls.

This German comedy is somewhat stolid in its humour, to put it charitably. Albers and Rühmann are lumpen, not convincing even as a bogus Holmes-Watson team yet not as roguishly appealing as they want to be—even when they break into a jaunty song while taking separate baths in their hotel suite. It's of interest in showing how Holmes was settling permanently into popular culture, especially in Germany. This 'Holmes' resembles other German film versions of the character—e.g.: stocky Hermann Speelmans in *Sherlock Holmes Die Graue Dame*—but looks little like the *Strand*-influenced version of the character of British and American films. The adventuress Ganymare sees through the imposture when she finds a receipt for Flint's Holmes disguise—which includes a loud-checked coat, a matching flat cap (not a deerstalker), a used violin case, and a straight pipe. It doesn't even run to the prop comedians usually wave about when posing as Holmes, a magnifying glass. There are surprisingly few Holmes-specific jokes and the film wouldn't be substantially different if the leads posed as any other detectives.

A running gag has a man (Paul Bildt) in an even louder check coat than Albers periodically observe the action and bark with laughter. He turns out to be Arthur Conan Doyle, approves of his fictional character being given life for a while, and wants the rights to write up their story. No one else in the film seems to think Holmes and Watson are fictional, though we see a story with a Doyle by-line and an Albers lookalike illustration. Doyle kept writing Holmes stories until his death in 1930, but stuck with the original Victorian setting. With very few exceptions—William Gillette's 1916 *Sherlock Holmes*, the first Basil Rathbone adventures in 1939—Holmes movies before the late 1950s assumed the detective's adventures took place in the present day. This is a partial exception. A few modern cars drive by in the street, but everyone dresses as if it were the Edwardian era. Director Karl Hartl is best remembered for the Albers-starring science fiction film *F.P.1 antwortet nicht* (1932). He also co-wrote this with Robert A. Stemmle.

LELÍCEK VE SLUZBÁCH SHERLOCKA HOLMESE (LELICEK IN THE SERVICES OF SHERLOCK HOLMES) (1939)

"Ah, Sherlock Holmes, you had a dog shop, didn't you?"

This Czech comedy—at heart a riff on *The Prisoner of Zenda*—opens with a montage of then-contemporary London, a Baker Street signpost, and Sherlock Holmes's nameplate. In 221B (with flashing neon signs outside the windows), a hawk-like Holmes (Mac Fric)—English-speaking but Czech-accented—broods in an armchair because he has yet to fulfill a commission from the Prime Minister of Puerto Rico to provide a double for King Fernando XXIII. Holmes is so concerned he has been playing his fiddle all night, annoying the neighbors. Poring over the Prague press, the Great Detective finds a Fernando lookalike—Frantisek Lelícek (Vlasta Burian), a mousta-chioed, bowler-hatted "eternal student."

Permanently broke and besieged by tradesmen (and his dentist) who want paying, Lelícek is trapped in his favourite café. Holmes, puffing a pipe and wearing the oversized tweed cap the character often sported instead of a deerstalker in European films of the 1930s, offers the boob any fee he likes to take the job. On a train with Holmes, instead of studying Spanish, Lelícek gives voice to a song he has written about "Rosita, Rosita, my Dearest Secret Love." This Puerto Rico is evidently a landlocked Ruritania-Graustarkian monarchy rather than the place the Sharks come from in *West Side Story*. In the Royal Palace, moustache-sporting, overdressed officials and dignitaries—including obvious rotters with silent movie villain looks—attend the elaborate levée (which involves taking a caged cockerel into the bed-chamber) of the paranoid sovereign. Here, Burian plays a different brand of feeble-minded (and, it has to be said, not very funny) char-acter. Holmes finally explains that the King is afraid of revolutionary assassins and needs someone to appear in public for him ("so the King is the expensive salami and I'm the cheap imitation?"). Even the dimwit sees the drawback—until Holmes explains that he can order anything he wants to eat.

The Queen (Lída Baarová) is annoyed at the King's cowardice and also that he has no romantic interest in her—obviously setting up later developments. Lelícek does schtick about giving medals to cacti, hat stands and stools to show he can act like a king, then a routine about eating meals in the manner of various national stereotypes (French, English). I assume from his filmography that Burian is some sort of Czech national treasure, but his basic, rather strained comic persona doesn't hold up well all these years on and in translation. Holmes introduces the King to his double ("I'm terribly sorry for him—you should have brought four at least, since this one won't survive till dinner") via the old split-screen trick. After appearing in public and disliking the national anthem, the fake king drags a smoking anar-chist bomb around on his train as he suggests to his shrinking cabinet that a contest be held to compose a new national anthem (it's been established that Lelícek is a song-writer, remember). The Queen is impressed with Lelícek's heroic handling of the bomb, which Holmes tosses into a pond, and tells her maid Conchita (E. Jansenova) that she likes the substitute monarch more than the authentic one.

Lelícek poses for postage photos, standing or sitting on a stuffed horse inside giant-sized stamp frames. Lelícek and the Queen's double appear in public, and they revert to silent movie flirt comedy while three solemn pianists hammer away at that dull national anthem—he orders them to play a merry tune, which sets the uniformed and liver-ied courtiers to foot-tapping as he sings the winning entry in the song contest. The court watch a bullfight (uncomically gory stock footage) and Lelícek gives the bull passionate support. Lelícek is summoned to the Queen's boudoir to help salve her migraine, leading to comedy seduction—like many comics, Burian's character is timid with wom-en when it comes down to it, but eventually willing. Emerging from the bedroom, Lelícek sees Holmes coaching the Queen's double and is confused as to which woman is which ("now, I have a headache").

All the wicked courtiers, plus some scarved, eye-patched gypsy types, scheme to kill the King ("not even his moustache will be left") with an exploding gramophone playing his contest-winning anthem. Holmes breaks into the plotters' lair with a brace of pistols, but is tricked into a cell and locked up. Lelícek fusses with the record, turn-ing back the needle just before the trigger passage in the tune—a comic riff on a suspense device from Hitchcock's *The Man Who Knew Too Much*—while Holmes needs to shoot at a switch to escape and (to build up suspense) misses eleven times before getting away in time to save the comedian. The Queen's double quits after the ex-plosion (which only injures the plotters, who have to be bandaged), and Lelícek admits he's made love to the real Queen—which irri-tates Holmes. News comes in that the real King is dead ("this means I should go and lie in the cemetery instead of him") and Lelícek, against Holmes's advice, decides to stay on as ruler of Puerto Rico because the Queen and the people love him. His first order is that Holmes should "take your pipe, hat and magnifying glass and find my double."

Not really a skit at the Great Detective's expense—though Holmes is lightly ridiculed in his introduction—but gets into the reference books for its unique Czech take on Conan Doyle's hero. Written by Václav Wasserman, from a novel by Hugo Vavris; directed by Carl Lamac. Fric also played Holmes in *Le Roi Bis*, a French version of the same script directed by Robert Beaudoin (probably on the same quite elaborate sets) with Pierre Bertin as the comedy lead.

✗

Kim Newman is a prolific, award-winning English writer and editor, who also acts, is a film critic, and a London broadcaster. Of his many novels and stories, one of the most famous is *Anno Dracula*.

CARNIVORY, DARWIN, AND DOYLE

by O'Neill Curatolo

"One of the great leaves of the flytrap, that had been shut and touchin' the ground as it lay, was slowly rolling back upon its hinges. There, lying like a child in its cradle, was Alabama Joe in the hollow of the leaf. The great thorns had been slowly driven through his heart as it shut on him. We could see as he'd tried to cut his way out, for there was a slit on the thick, fleshy leaf, an' his bowie was in his hand; but it had smothered him first."

—Sir Arthur Conan Doyle, *The American's Tale* (1880)

Sherlock Holmes aficionados are familiar with the first appearance of Holmes and Watson in the 1887 novel *A Study in Scarlet*. In the context of the whole of the Holmes canon, the section of this work that occurs on the arid plains of the American West seems oddly anomalous, taking place as it does thousands of miles from Victorian London. It turns out that Arthur Conan Doyle had a long-standing interest in the American West. In 1880, seven years before the first appearance of Holmes and Watson, the twenty-one-year-old Doyle published a mystery/thriller story set there.

The American's Tale is of interest in at least two respects. First, it is written largely in Doyle's version of western cowboy slang. One must assume that he invented this exaggerated *lingua americana* based on the dialogue in pulp novels he read. The second point of interest is the unusual way in which one of the characters dies—killed by a giant venus fly-trap.

From 1876 to 1881 Doyle studied medicine at the University of Edinburgh and during this period he also studied botany at The Royal Botanic Garden. Thus he would have been familiar with the extensive experimental work on carnivorous plants carried out by Charles Darwin, who commenced this work in 1860, the year after he published *On the Origin of Species*. Darwin characterized the unusual traits of these plants into three aspects: capture of the prey, digestion of the prey, and absorption of the digested material. He carried out large numbers of experiments aimed at understanding the physiological and biochemical details of these three aspects and in 1875 published this major work in his 462-page book *Insectivorous Plants*.

Darwin reported that once the carnivorous plant has captured its prey, it secretes an acidic mixture of degradative enzymes similar to those in the human gastrointestinal tract. These enzymes slowly, over the course of days, digest the prey. Not a quick way to die, to say the least. The inner surface of the various traps is also, like the human GI tract, capable of absorbing the soluble products of the plant's digestion of the prey. Of course the anatomical similarity to the human GI tract is only conceptual, but the biochemistry of the individual digestive enzymes is quite similar. Darwin's groundbreaking work has been extended over the subsequent century and a half by generations of scientists. In 2017 Kenji Fukushima and colleagues published the DNA sequence of the entire genome of the carnivorous pitcher plant *Caphalotus follicularis*, in addition to the identity of the genes controlling the component activities of carnivory.

Of course it is the trapping mechanism that captures the attention of the non-biologist public, and carnivorous plants have evolved a variety of approaches to predation. The major types are the active and passive flypapers (the sundews, e.g. *Droseria*), the spring-traps (venus fly-trap, e.g. *Dionaea*) and the pitchers with slippery walls (pitcher plants, e.g. *Sarracenia*). In *The American's Tale*, Doyle chose to utilize the fearsome spring-trap, which seems the most actively malevolent. The hinged-leaf of the venus fly-trap has a bivalve shape like a clam, with trigger hairs on the inner leaf surface. When prey touches two hairs, the hinged-leaf closes quickly, trapping the prey, then slowly compresses to make a tight compartment in which most prey can move only minimally. Then digestive juices are secreted into the compartment containing the prey.

The flypapers comprise a variety of leaf designs that have one thing in common—hairs on the surface with droplets of a sticky substance on their tips. When prey gets stuck on the leaf surface of an active flypaper, the leaf slowly curls around the hapless prey and slow digestion begins.

The pitcher plant possesses the most efficient of the trapping mechanisms. This carnivore has leaves which curl and seal to form a Champagne flute-shaped pitcher with a slippery nectar-coated mouth which in some cases also secretes the paralytic alkaloid coniine. When a crawling or flying insect samples the nectar on the slippery lip of the pitcher, it becomes disoriented by the coniine and falls into the long flute-shaped pitcher. The interior walls of the pitcher are coated with a slippery waxy substance and have downward facing hairs, making it all but impossible for the prey to climb up and out. Digestive juices are secreted at the bottom of the pitcher, where the exoskeletons of digested insects eventually accumulate. Some pitcher plants grow relatively large, and hapless mice and frogs have been known to fall in and be killed and digested. (A reader who wishes to witness such rodent and amphibian extermination can do so by computer-searching "mouse pitcher plant" and "frog pitcher plant.")

Doyle chose the hinge-leafed fly-trap mechanism to end the life of Alabama Joe in *The American's Tale*. Is it feasible that a gigantic man-eating fly-trap of this type could exist? The general scientific consensus is that the osmotic mechanism that operates the hinged-leaf trap is insufficient for moving large man-size leaves. Regardless, in Doyle's Victorian-era story a giant fly-trap certainly killed Alabama Joe. And a century later real-world scientific constraints did not prevent the existence of the kitschy extraterrestrial man-eating plant Audrey Jr. in the 1960 film *Little Shop of Horrors* or the mobile man-eating plants in the 1962 film *The Day of the Triffids*.

O'Neill Curatolo is a biophysicist who holds 36 US Patents. His suspense novel *Campanilismo* (2013) chronicles the activities of drug industry physicians and scientists in ethically murky waters in New Jersey, Kuala Lumpur, and Malaysian Borneo. He has just published a sequel titled *Too Many Hats: Herbal Medicine and The Mob* (2018), about which Kirkus Reviews said, "An entertaining and illuminating romp through interconnected and delightfully suspect organizations."

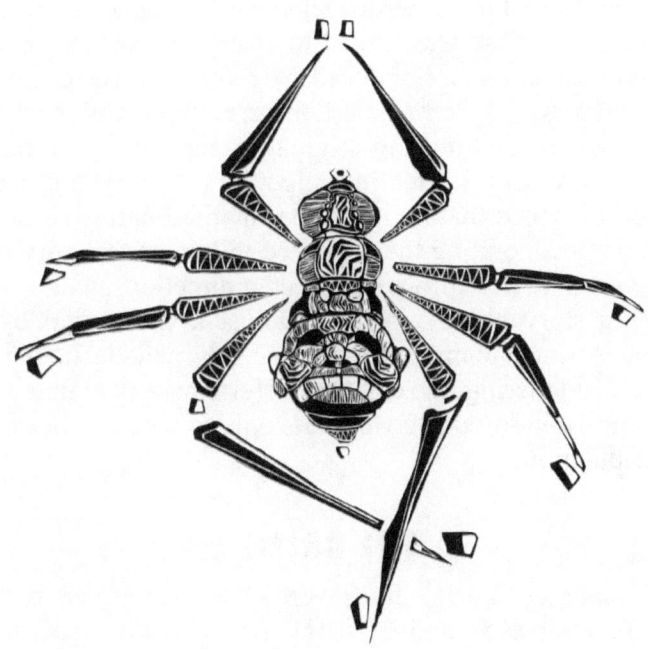

"SOMEDAY THE TRUTH WILL COME OUT":

THE LEMBERGER FAMILY AND THE MURDER THAT STUNNED WISCONSIN

by Chris Chan

INTRODUCTION

In 1911 a little girl was kidnapped from her home in Madison and brutally murdered. It would become one of the most famous crimes in Wisconsin's history. Over the next few decades, two different men would be accused of the crime, one of whom would go to jail and become the focus of a massive exoneration campaign. A dramatic courtroom battle captured the imagination of the community. The victim's family was attacked by journalists, community members and even a prominent Ivy League professor. Wisconsin's state government was embroiled in numerous legal battles connected to the cases for years and the case was linked to scandals with the potential to explode political careers. For decades devotees of true crime thought that they knew who killed Annie Lemberger and why. Nearly three-quarters of a century after the original crime, Mark Lemberger, the nephew of the victim, started investigating the crime and uncovered overlooked evidence that knocked the standard narrative of the case upside-down, exonerating the supposed villain of the story and casting blame in some heretofore unexpected directions.

This is a story about violence against a child, trial by media, corruption, perjury, community outrage, journalistic incompetence, government blundering, the creation of false historical narratives and how one family endured a terrible loss only to face another powerful, lifelong tribulation.

THE CRIME

The Lemberger family's lives were changed forever on the night between September 5th and 6th, 1911. Annie Lemberger, just seven years old, disappeared from her bedroom. Her mother Magdeline made the discovery the next morning, later explaining that, "I put Annie to bed about ten o'clock last night. My two little boys slept in the same room. Annie slept right near the window. This morning when I got up to get Mr. Lemberger's breakfast, Annie was gone."[1] She immediately sent her husband Martin to call the police and the authorities launched their search for the kidnapped girl. The Madison newspapers immediately latched onto the story, the story soon spread to the national news and the community united in anxiety for Annie's safety.[2]

Days passed without any news of Annie. Bloodhounds, community volunteers and even a medium failed to produce results.[3] The Lemberger family hoped for the best during this time, as thousands of phone calls poured in to the authorities and the local newspapers called for justice. After three days of worrying and media frenzy, on the morning of Saturday, September 9th, Annie's nude corpse was found floating in Lake Monona.

While the major question was "Who kidnapped and killed Annie?," some people were asking the additional question, "Why was Annie kidnapped and murdered?" Grant Brightman, a journalist, commented, "The question of a motive is still puzzling everyone working on the case. There seems to be no reason why the daughter of parents too poor to pay a ransom and with no wealthy friends and no enemies should be carried out in a manner so filled with risk to the intruder."[4]

The newspapers whipped up community outrage with headlines like "THE FIEND MUST BE FOUND" and the community demanded that the culprit be caught and jailed.[5] The unprecedented nature of the crime added fuel to the fire—this was the first time that the kidnapping and murder of a child shattered the calm of Madison. With no forensic evidence and no witnesses, the authorities started combing the neighborhood for clues. They found their first likely suspect three houses away from the Lembergers in John A. Johnson, nicknamed "Dogskin" thanks to his being suspected of stealing a tanned canine hide. Johnson bore a reputation for being a ne'er-do-well, having

---

1   August Derleth, *Wisconsin Murders* (Sauk City, Wisconsin: Mycroft and Moran, 1968), 152.
2   "Stole Child As She Slept," *New York Times* on the Web, 7 September 1921.
3   Mark Lemberger, *Crime of Magnitude: The Murder of Little Annie* (Madison, Wisconsin: Prairie Oak Press, 1993), 6-11.
4   Derleth, 153.
5   Lemberger, 15.

been arrested for various crimes in the past, such as failure to look after his wife and daughters and was also a former asylum patient.[6]

Johnson first drew attention due to his extreme interest in the case. He lurked around the Lemberger home during the days after the kidnapping (not innately suspicious in itself, as hundreds of people stopped by the Lemberger house during this time to sympathize, offer help, snoop around and swap theories). When Johnson repeatedly interrupted the autopsy, the coroner Matt Lynch thought it worthwhile to interview him.[7]

At this point narratives of the story start to diverge. In August Derleth's *Wisconsin Murders*, Johnson was given the third degree, relentlessly pressured by the police to confess and angry crowds threatened his life.[8] Contemporaneous news accounts mention Johnson's alleged fear of the police, but also assert that he was faking insanity.[9] In *Crime of Magnitude*, Mark Lemberger argues that the police behaved appropriately and disagrees with Johnson's assertion that he feared being lynched by an angry mob and therefore considered himself safer in a secure prison. Johnson did confess to Annie's murder. With Johnson's statement, a judge sentenced him to life imprisonment without a trial, but almost immediately, Johnson started proclaiming that he was pressured into confessing and that he was an innocent man.[10]

It was too late to take back the confession, so Johnson was stuck in prison, though the controversy over the case was just beginning. Unlike many less prominent crimes, the city of Madison never forgot the case and many citizens discussed Annie's kidnapping for years after Johnson's conviction. Rumors circulated that Johnson was completely innocent and that the Lembergers were involved in their own daughter's death, but the authorities did not take the accusations seriously.[11] It was not until a crusading lawyer entered the picture that the case would take a dramatic turn.

OLE STOLEN FOR THE DEFENSE

A decade passed. Johnson being locked away in jail did nothing to stop the rumors that continued to circulate around Madison. Numerous people were convinced of Johnson's innocence and a large

6   Lemberger, 15-16.
7   Derleth, 156.
8   Derleth, 156-157.
9   "Child-Slayer Confesses," *New York Times* on the Web, 14 September 1911.
10   Derleth, 158-160.
11   Derleth, 162.

segment of the city's population demanded further investigation. No real momentum occurred until Madison lawyer Ole Stolen took up the mantle of Johnson's legal representative.

Stolen was an ambitious man with dreams of working his way up the state judiciary. After seeing an anonymous letter insisting that Johnson was wrongfully convicted, Stolen decided to take the case. Stolen may have been inspired by multiple motives. Though he presented himself as being wholly concerned with justice, his ambitious side probably calculated that the trial could be used as publicity in order to advance his own career. Additionally, if Johnson was exonerated and released, he would very likely have received a substantial settlement from the state government and Stolen would have been entitled to a significant share of that.[12]

Stolen eventually got Governor Blaine to grant Johnson a pardon hearing on Monday, September 26, 1921.[13] During the first four and a half days in court, Stolen produced very little exculpatory evidence towards Johnson. However, when Stolen brought his final witness to the stand on September 29, 1921, everything changed.[14] Mae Sorenson, a scrub woman working at a theatre who claimed to be a friend of the Lembergers, started testifying in a raspy voice, declaring that she'd been in the Lembergers's home on the morning Annie disappeared. Sorenson and Stolen kept the courtroom in thrall as she described how the Lembergers's eldest son Louis told her that Annie's father Martin was enraged that night, eventually beating Annie with a beer bottle, causing her to crack her head against the stove. Sorenson elaborated on how Annie was put to bed and was later found dead and Magdeline and Louis Lemberger hired an unnamed black man to dispose of the body. Sorenson claimed that Martin bullied her into silence and she kept quiet for years out of fear of violent reprisals from Martin.[15]

The courtroom was blindsided by Sorenson's revelations. The prosecutor was so taken aback that his follow-up questioning was perfunctory. All of the spectators believed that they saw the truth revealed in the most dramatic manner possible and the attendees stood and applauded Sorenson as she finished her testimony.[16]

---

12   Lemberger, 266-267.
13   Lemberger, 70.
14   Lemberger, 89.
15   "Lemberger Denies Killing Daughter," *New York Times* on the Web, 7 October 1921.
16   Lemberger, 118.

The Lembergers came to Johnson's pardon hearing in the hopes of seeing him sent back to prison for life. Instead, by the end of the hearing Dogskin was expected to be released soon and Martin and Magdeline Lemberger, along with their eldest son Louis, were sent to jail. Stolen himself swore out their warrants, though in his exuberance, he charged the Lembergers with perjury before they even testified.[17]

Aside from Louis, there were four surviving children in the Lemberger family. George Lemberger, their grandfather, cared for them while their parents and eldest sibling were imprisoned. George carried a gun for protection, but the weapon was ineffective against the verbal assault that his granddaughter Marie would suffer over the telephone. The fourteen-year-old girl picked up the phone and was met by a torrent of verbal abuse by an anonymous female. The caller ranted about the iniquity of the Lembergers and Marie fainted before she could replace the receiver. The strain of her family's legal woes and the seething hatred expressed by some members of the community destroyed Marie's health and a year later the teenager was dead, officially by "heart failure due to exhaustion." Much later, Magdeline privately mourned, saying, "What no one knows is that this whole thing cost our family both our daughters."[18]

Parents and son sat in a jail cell for some time before Martin was released on a $10,000 bail and Magdeline and Louis's bonds were set at a thousand dollars apiece.[19] The charges against Madgeline and Louis were finally dismissed due in part to the fact that they were arrested at Stolen's instigation. When Magdeline and Louis spoke at the trial, it was not under oath, so there could be no perjury. Stolen's work was so slipshod that he even wrongly addressed Magdeline as "Annie" on the arrest warrant. On October 25, 1921, with no legally supportable charge of perjury, Magdeline and Louis were set free with all charges dismissed.[20]

Martin would spend much more time in the criminal justice system. He faced a preliminary hearing just two days after Christmas of 1921.[21] During Johnson's pardon hearing, the state was not prepared to confront Stolen's surprise witness. In contrast, Martin's defense attorney Carl Hill was a skilled cross-examiner and challenged all the

---

17   Lemberger, 119-120, 131.

18   Lemberger, 127.
19   Lemberger, 128.
20   Lemberger, 131.
21   Lemberger, 134.

evidence against his client.[22] Even Special Prosecutor Ralph Jackman admitted that, "The only testimony which would warrant a charge of murder is that of Mae Sorenson."[23]

Based on the limited evidence and Mae Sorenson's description of events, Jackman concluded that the only suitable charge would be one of fourth-degree manslaughter, usually used in intoxicated driving fatalities. The statute of limitations on that charge was a decade, which meant it was too late to charge Martin Lemberger. Martin was therefore released on January 9, 1922, safe from legal repercussions but not the ire of the community.[24]

Magdeline tearfully described her feelings to a reporter, saying, "I can't understand how people who knew nothing of the case could say the things they did... Martin's trial has cost us $3,000 [This equates to $43,665 in 2017 dollars].[25] Just think what $3,000 would mean to my little girl and boys. And we have not the money. We have had to borrow it ... It will take bitter toil to pay even the interest."[26]

Many people thought that Martin should have stood up for himself in court in order to publicly prove his innocence, but if he pursued that course of action, the legal fees for an extended trial would have dug the Lembergers into a financial hole from which they might have never escaped.[27] Even if Martin was cleared in court, he would not have convinced all of Madison of his innocence and there was no guarantee that the verdict would have been in his favor. The Lembergers were free, but left struggling to pay off a massive mortgage and surrounded by thousands of people who believed that he escaped justice for murdering his own daughter, though there were plenty of Madisonians who believed in their innocence.

BOB BISHOP OF THE CHICAGO DAILY TIMES ON THE CASE

The Lembergers were free from legal reprisals, but the shadow of public condemnation still haunted them. Interestingly, though the family moved away from the house where Annie was kidnapped long before, they never tried to move away to a different city, where they could start their lives again in relative anonymity. They remained in

22   Lemberger, 140-143.
23   Lemberger, 143-144.
24   Lemberger, 144-145.
25   "US Inflation Calculator," http://www.usinflationcalculator. com, (12 May 2017).
26   Lemberger, 145-146.
27   Derleth, 166-167.

Madison, living near where Annie's body was found in Lake Monona. A large portion of the population believed that they got away with murder and Johnson supporters campaigned to get financial compensation for Johnson's incarceration (their efforts would meet with some success in 1935, when after years of controversy and wrangling amongst factions in the government, Johnson was awarded a small pension for the rest of his life).[28]

Over the next several years numerous people would write about the case. The most prominent chronicler was Ole Stolen, who wrote a three-part series of articles about the case for the popular true crime magazine *Master Detective*, portraying himself in a heroic light.[29] Over the coming decades Stolen would show these articles to everybody who asked him about the case and they would become the most commonly consulted resource about the death of Annie Lemberger. When Edwin M. Borchard, a law professor at Yale, wrote the book *Convicting the Innocent*, a collection of sixty-five essays about people who were found guilty of murder and then cleared later, he relied heavily on Stolen's coverage of the case and painted the Lembergers in a very dark light.[30]

In 1932 Bob Bishop of the *Chicago Daily News* decided to write about the murder case. He travelled to Madison and interviewed Stolen and Johnson's new lawyer Herb Siggelko. When he mentioned that he wanted to interview the Lembergers to hear their side of the story, Stolen and other Johnson supporters insisted that the Lemberger family were dangerous criminals and that Bishop would interview them at his own peril. Despite the warnings Bishop decided that it was important to be thorough and he went to seek out the Lembergers's side of the story, accompanied by a photographer/bodyguard.[31]

When he spoke to them, he found the Lembergers to be sympathetic people, unlikely to be heartless killers who allowed an innocent man to rot in jail. Their house was filled with pictures of Annie and they were adamant about their innocence, which led Bishop to wonder: might the Lembergers be telling the truth?

Bishop turned to new technology to investigate further. The lie detector was a recent invention that some excited criminologists believed would revolutionize the art of identifying guilty suspects. (Today lie detectors are never used as acceptable evidence in court,

28   Lemberger, 264-268.
29   Lemberger, 244-246, 257.
30   Edwin M. Borchard, *Convicting the Innocent: Sixty-Five Actual Errors of Criminal Justice* (Garden City, New York: Garden City Publishing Company, Inc., 1932), 110-119.
31   Lemberger, 255-256.

since they are not completely reliable and mistakes can be made for various reasons.) On January 5, 1933, the separately questioned Lembergers passed their combined approximately four hours of exams. "Dogskin" Johnson's tests produced inconclusive results, though he reportedly lied on some possibly innocuous matters. Mae Sorenson was tested the next day and failed. When confronted with her test results, Sorenson eventually broke down and fully recanted her testimony, claiming some unnamed man bribed her to lie—but never paid her the agreed-upon $500.[32]

MARK LEMBERGER INVESTIGATES

Very little changed after Bishop's articles exonerating the Lembergers were released. The Madison newspapers did not acknowledge this work (Mark Lemberger would later theorize that they were embarrassed at being scooped by an out-of-town reporter and wanted to protect Stolen) and as the ensuing campaign to have the state recompense Johnson for his incarceration illustrated, the general public and the major figures in Madison's political scene were unaware of the new investigation's results. In the late 1940's a magazine printed a retrospective on the case identifying Martin as the killer. Armed with the *Chicago Daily News* articles, Magdalene sued for libel and eventually won a substantial cash settlement, which she shared with her surviving children. She used her portion to build a monument to her daughter.[33] Despite these words, the case slowly faded from public memory as everybody involved with the case passed away one by one and more recent crimes and scandals captured the public imagination.

Despite the case's fading profile the Lemberger family never forgot and never spoke of the case in public or private, either. In 1985, Mark Lemberger, the grandson of Martin and Magdeline, rediscovered his family's history through a retrospective newspaper article and grew fascinated with the case. He knew his family believed in his grandfather's innocence, but if Martin was not culpable, who was?

Mark Lemberger asserts that he did not start his historical investigation with the intention of clearing his grandparents's names.

"Exonerating my grandparents... was never much in my mind. The [family] name was fine when I was growing up. I knew my folks to be moral and good citizens and it never occurred to me that it could be otherwise. I was 34 or so when I really first heard the story and I pretty well knew who I was.

---

32   Lemberger, 260-263.
33   Lemberger, 304.

What compelled me to know what happened was the quality of the mystery. I'm not a true crime fan and never was... This opus would have been much easier if my name was not the same as some of the characters."[34]

When conducting his historical investigation, Mark Lemberger gathered up as much evidence as possible. Nearly three quarters of a century elapsed, leaving much potential information inaccessible. Certain newspapers went out of business and their old editions were unarchived. It was only due to the relentless preservation efforts of his grandmother that Mark Lemberger was able to gain access to contemporaneous news coverage and other critical articles connected to the case. He explained,

> "My primary source was a huge scrapbook Magdeline Lemberger kept from 1911 to 1952. In it she assembled hundreds of newspaper articles, book chapters, etc. I got access to her database in 1985 when the articles were copied. She added nothing of her own besides a bit of marginalia but when I reassembled all these articles I had a broad understanding of the story. All the principals were dead, including my Dad, who was born five years after Annie's death."[35]

It soon became apparent to Mark Lemberger that if he was to make sense of the evidence, proper organization was critical. He reflected,

> "One thing that can't be over-emphasized; who best understands the timeline wins the case. I have large sheets of paper headed DAY I, II etc. starting with Annie's disappearance. This sprang from Magdeline's having kept the original reporting. This data was scrambled, misinterpreted, remembered wrong and lied about at the Pardon Hearing... When I came to understand the Grant Brightman error [The cited date of Annie's kidnapping was a day off in one report and Stolen never caught this mistake and Mae Sorenson gave the same wrong date in her testimony.] over the dates and how Ole Stolen believed it correct and infected/confused all his witnesses, then I could reconstruct his briefing of his witnesses and realize just how careless Ole was. With these DAY # sheets I could trace each cop, JAJ and each Lemberger through the week of the crime. Immensely useful."[36]

34   Mark Lemberger, email message to author, March 13, 2017.
35   Mark Lemberger, Facebook message to author, March 9, 2017.
36   Mark Lemberger, email message to author, March 15, 2017.

Mark came to see Stolen as both the most interesting figure in the case and as a kind of personal nemesis. At one point Mark hung a picture of Stolen up to inspire him as he pored over records. Mark quipped that, "Folks used to say of Stolen, "He was nothing if not dogged," and Mark would tell Stolen's photograph, "I'll show you dogged.""[37]

Throughout his research Mark Lemberger spoke with many experts in law enforcement and criminal investigation. He explained:

> "I could inveigle many experts to confer with me. I couldn't pay them so I would say, "Give me five minutes to tell you about this crime. If you've ever heard of one like it, I'll never bother you again." Usually I'd hear something like, "Son, I've given 45,000 polygraph exams and I've heard it all, but go ahead." Five minutes later they invariably said, "Go on." This was after most of the research was done so my questions were few and sharp. That helped a great deal. I got an FBI profiler (that was kind of in its infancy in 1990), a medical examiner, prison psychologist, federal prosecutor, etc."[38]

The vital clue was in the autopsy reports, which now only existed in Magdeline's personal archive. In Mae Sorenson's testimony she claimed that Annie was bludgeoned to death, but the original forensic examination told a different story. The head wounds were insufficient to cause death and a bluish tinge to Annie's skin led to another conclusion—death by suffocation. If that was the case, then Mae Sorenson's testimony was unquestionably perjured. If Mae lied, then someone fed her details and coached her in order to create a convincing narrative. Mark concluded that there was only one person who could have done that: Ole Stolen. Mark Lemberger became further suspicious of Stolen's narrative of the case as he discovered that many public records connected to the case were missing crucial evidence. "Over several years it became clear that someone preceded me in the many different official archives and taken most of the original records. Some of them were only accessible to someone with a court order so it had to have been Ole Stolen."[39]

---

37   Jennie Kaufman, "Murder and the Family Story," 3 September 2015, https://blogs.ancestry.com/ancestry/2015/09/03/murder-and-the-family-story/ (14 May 2017).

38   Mark Lemberger, email message to author, March 15, 2017.

39   Mark Lemberger, Facebook messages to author, March 9-10, 2017.

For decades Stolen presented himself as a crusader for justice—a precursor to Perry Mason, as well as the chief historian of the case. Mark's investigation stripped away Stolen's halo and cast a far more sinister light on the man. Further inquiry proved that Stolen's later career was less than distinguished. Stolen embarrassed himself with odd pronouncements about the prevalence of venereal disease in Madison, lost his judgeship after being caught in a corruption scandal connected to bootleggers and after numerous mostly unsuccessful attempts at rehabilitating his public image, died in obscurity and relative poverty.[40]

According to Mark, Stolen latched onto the case, bribed Mae Sorenson to lie and took control of the media narrative in order to present himself as a heroic figure, thereby advancing his career. When asked why he thought that Stolen might have suborned perjury in order to exonerate Johnson, Mark theorized that, "Once he was morally certain he could rationalize doing evil that a greater good might happen. That Johnson's liberation would reward him with his ultimate ambition would seem fair to him."[41]

Mark's ruminations on the man who ruined his family's reputation led to his conclusion that Stolen always believed he was the good guy.

> "I'm fascinated by the question "Did Ole honestly believe Johnson innocent?" I'm quite sure he did. And everything he did had that as its point of departure. Nothing in my grandma's scrapbook referenced Ole's fall from grace and disbarment. What does that tell us? I called older attorneys in the Dane County Bar in 1988 and one of the gents mentioned that Ole was disbarred and that he mentored a young attorney into his firm. That attorney William Bradford Smith was still practicing. I called him and asked if I could speak to him about Ole Stolen. The first thing he told me was, "I loved that man." "Great!" I said, "would you defend him?" "Yes," I was told. So I laid out my evidence and charges and he ultimately agreed Ole was almost certainly being blackmailed for suborning perjury. But I knew Ole was affable, warm-hearted and passionate and saw much evidence of all this. Yet he was center stage in his own Greek tragedy of hubris, then nemesis."[42]

Having provided exculpatory evidence for his grandfather and explaining how the evidence against him was falsified, Lemberger

---

40   Lemberger, 167-238, 289-292.

41   Mark Lemberger, email message to author, March 12, 2017.

42   Mark Lemberger, Facebook message to author, March 10, 2017.

reviewed the records of the case and found out that there was more to the story of "Dogskin" Johnson than was told in previous histories of the case. Johnson was previously convicted for the sexual assault of minors, attempted train derailment and spousal abandonment.[43] Upon discrediting the many attempts at rehabilitating Johnson's character, Lemberger concludes in *Crime of Magnitude* that the authorities got the right man the first time. He argues, "Johnson... was a psychopath... He was a man without a conscience and a highly skilled liar."[44]

Lemberger's work effectively clears his family name and though he has provided a significant amount of evidence illustrating that Johnson was guilty all along, there are some online sleuths who still believe in Johnson's innocence and others who believe in Martin's guilt. Others reflect on the lingering possibility that some unknown party might have been the murderer.[45] Lemberger observed that prior to *Crime of Magnitude*'s publication, "Ole Stolen owned the story" of Annie's murder.[46] That is no longer the case.

CONCLUSION

For much of the first half of the twentieth century the Lemberger case was the most famous case of a murdered child in America, overshadowed only by the Lindbergh baby kidnapping. Today, the case is largely forgotten, save for some Wisconsinites with long memories and for some true crime aficionados. The case provides many important lessons applicable to contemporary society. In recent years, some high-profile true crime entertainment productions have provoked outrage by claiming that miscarriages of justice have been done, but the Lemberger case illustrates that there may be more to some of these stories than many true crime fans believe.

Mark Lemberger recently reflected on how the case not only illustrated one man's political corruption, but how the effort to clear

---

43   Lemberger, 293-301.

44   Lemberger, 299.

45   "Dastardly Dads from the Archives," 18 August 2009, http://dastardlydads.blogspot.com/search?q=lemberger (14 May 2017). Note: the narrative of events in this post is full of errors and omissions. "John Johnson," June 2008, http://vots.altervista.org/WI/Johnson.html (14 May 2017). Jennifer Hoff, "Cold Case Wisconsin: Who Killed Little Annie Lemberger?," 20 November 2013, http://www.channel3000.com/news/local-news/cold-case-wisconsin-who-killed-little-annie-lemberger/158902658 (14 May 2017).

46   Kaufman.

and compensate Johnson may have corrupted the state government as well.

Think about how much history is PR. In this case politicians were far more likely to be damaged if they did NOT support the "Justice for Johnson" bandwagon. [Governor and later presidential candidate] Phil LaFollette was castigated for denying JAJ the big bucks and was accused of having "a tin veneered conscience." Ole drove this campaign for fame, money and personal vindication. He completely won the PR campaign, owned the story and wrote the history... repeatedly.

So it would have remained except that my grandmother, while mourning the death of her seven year-old daughter, while being considered a truly evil woman by half her townsfolk, found, assembled and preserved all the information she possibly could on this tragedy.

Why?

Her son George Sebastian Lemberger, thirteen months old when Annie was killed said to me at a lunch several years into my research, "My mother always said someday the truth will come out."

And so it did.[47]

Chris Chan is a historian, educator, and writer from Milwaukee, Wisconsin. He works as a researcher and "International Goodwill Ambassador" for Agatha Christie Ltd. His work has appeared in *The Strand Magazine*, *Gilbert!*, *Serial Magazine*, and *The Wisconsin Magazine of History*.

---

47   Mark Lemberger, email message to author, March 11, 2017.

DR. WATSON AND TRUE FACTS

by Bruce Harris

News coverage about facts is pervasive. Yet, the topic is, as the saying goes, nothing new under the sun. Sherlock Holmes's chronicler, Dr. John H. Watson was ahead of his time on many fronts.

The late Aubrey C. Roberts is unduly critical of Dr. Watson.[1] Roberts first questions Watson's judgment for writing "The Adventure of the Second Stain" (SECO). He also wonders why, after enumerating seven blunders made by Sherlock Holmes, Watson remarks, "My mind filled with admiration for this extraordinary man." Although not as harsh, Nathan L. Bengis also raises questions about the case. He questions why Holmes did not admit his mistake regarding the death of Eduardo Lucas, and more specifically, asks why Watson did not resort to the familiar, "I told you so" retort.[2]

Interestingly, Roger Butters raises a similar question regarding "The Adventure of the Speckled Band" (SPEC).[3] He is one of many tackling the identity of Dr. Grimesby Roylott's swamp adder. Butters is convinced that the cobra is the snake in question. However he points out the following limitation to his theory. "The cobra is one of the few snakes that almost anyone, including Watson, could be trusted to recognize. Why, if he knew perfectly well that it was a cobra, did he report the Holmes classification, 'swamp adder' without comment?"[4]

Two distinct cases, yet Watson finds himself in two similar, uncomfortable circumstances. In each, what he sees and knows to be correct is contrary to what Holmes perceives as reality. In SECO, Holmes tells Watson the murder of Eduardo Lucas must be related to the stolen document, when in reality it is not. And, Watson knows it to be a falsehood. In SPEC, Holmes identifies the snake as a swamp adder, a fictitious beast. Watson knows it to be a cobra. What to do?

---

1   Aubrey C. Roberts," The Real Second Stain: A Tarnished Idol", *Baker Street Journal*, Vol. 32, No. 4, (Dec. 1982): pp. 227-229.

2   Nathan L. Bengis, "Sherlock Stays After School", *Illustrious Client's Second Case Book*, J.N. Williamson, ed., The Illustrious Clients, Indianapolis, IN, 1949, pp. 72-78.

3   Roger Butters, *First Person Singular*, Vantage Press, New York, 1984.

4   Roger Butters, pp. 84.

Watson's behavior is consistent in both cases. He does not challenge Holmes in either instance. Rather he subtly and deliberately complicates matters. By so doing he acts quite rationally. This will be demonstrated shortly.

It is not mere coincidence that in the text of both cases Watson chooses the enigmatic term *true facts* (it is used twice in SECO). The only other time *true facts* is found in the entire Holmes Canon is in "The Adventure of the Naval Treaty." And in that instance Watson quoted from SECO! What is behind its usage? It is an unnecessarily complex, meaningless and redundant phrase. The adjective, *true*, is superfluous. According to Webster, the definition of "in fact" is, "in truth."[5]

"Such are the *true facts* of the death of Dr. Grimsby Roylott, of Stoke Moran," writes Dr. Watson in SPEC. As opposed to what other type of facts, one could ask? Alternative? Despite Watson's declaration, many have argued the accuracy of Watson's account of SPEC. Leslie Klinger cites nine other authors (in addition to Butters's cobra hypothesis) speculating about the identity of the snake.[6] There is even a school of thought that argues the snake had nothing to do with Roylott's death.[7]

By employing complex phrases and storylines, Watson's behavior is actually a quite typical human response. A classical psychological experiment conducted by Alex Bavelas in the 1950's found that people resort to subtle and complete explanations as a means of coping with situations where their own perceptions are contradicted by the feedback of others. In other words, these subjects are searching for an order or explanation to coincide with what they have witnessed. Or as Paul Watzlawick puts it, "… Once a tentative explanation has taken hold of our minds, information to the contrary may produce not corrections, but elaborations of the explanation."[8] Internal conflict leads to what psychologist Leon Festinger has called cognitive dissonance.[9] People usually try to reduce the dissonance by somehow

---

5   Henry Bosley Woolf, ed., *Webster's New Collegiate Dictionary*, G.&C.Merriam Company, Springfield, MA, 1977, pp. 410.

6   Leslie S. Klinger, ed. *The Adventures of Sherlock Holmes* (The Sherlock Holmes Reference Library), Gasogene Books, Indianapolis, IN, 1978, pp. 181-205.

7   T.F. Foss and J.M. Linsenmeyer, "Look to the Lady", *Baker Street Journal*, Vol. 27, No. 2, pp. 79-85.

8   Paul Watzlawick, *How Real is Real?* Vintage Books, New York, 1977.

9   Leon Festinger, *A Theory of Cognitive Dissonance*, Row Peterson, Everston, IL, 1957.

explaining away the inconsistency. Rather than stand up to Holmes, Watson searches for other ways or means to eliminate his discomfort and restore internal order. He adjusts by concocting elaborate and complex explanations and employs unrealistic terminology to fit Holmes's view of the world. This extends to Sherlockian scholars as well. A classic example is George J. McCormack's, "A Second Look at The Second Stain".[10] McCormack accuses Lady Hilda Trelawney Hope of murdering the scoundrel Lucas, an elaborate theory that fits nicely with Holmes's view of the case rather than the case presented by Watson. Perhaps Robert Kernish summed it up best. "We shall probably never know the *true facts* of "The Adventure of the Second Stain" or the part Holmes played in that affair."[11]

✗

Bruce Harris is the author of *Sherlock Holmes and Doctor Watson: ABout Type*. His Sherlockian articles have appeared in *The Baker Street Journal*, *The Sherlock Holmes Journal*, *Canadian Holmes*, and *Mystery Weekly Magazine*. An Oscar Meunier Sherlock Holmes bust sits on his desk.

---

10   George J. McCormack. "A Second Look at the Second Stain", *Baker Street Journal*, Vol. 42, No. 1, 38-41.

11   Robert Kernish, "The Curious Case of the Second Stain", *Baker Street Journal*, Vol. 16, No. 3, (Sept. 1966): pp. 173-174.

THE RED-FACED LEAGUE

by Hal Charles

Saturday night while the winter snow fell, Kelly Locke was poring over her computerized notes and pictures for her testimony at the
Mary Sutherland trial the coming Monday when she heard an email
ping in. Tired but curious, the co-anchor of *The Six O'clock News*
clicked on the new arrival.

"Ms. Locke," read the message, "please excuse the lateness of this
important request, but I have a weekend project that will not attain
its true potential without your presence at my estate, Thule. If I have
piqued your interest sufficiently, please reply immediately. I will then
messenger you $25,000 (for you/your favorite charity) tonight, a car
will pick you up at 8:00 a.m. tomorrow morning and you will receive
up to an additional $100,000 when the process, a solution and dinner,
is complete. Honorably yours, Jonathan Valiant."

The only things that Kelly knew about her emailer was that he
headed up the very successful Valiant Fund and that he owned a man-
sion north of the city. In all her years at Channel Four, she had been
able to secure interviews with three Presidents, but not the man whose
wealth and prestige put him in the lofty club whose membership consisted of such giants as Bill Gates and Warren Buffett. Valiant's desire
for privacy had become as legendary as that of bygone titan Howard
Hughes.

For Kelly, winter brought not only the bad weather but doldrums
when, despite the largest television audience in the metropolitan area,
she felt cut off from humanity. She clicked back up her notes on the
computer. Who was she kidding? She was just over-studying because
she was bored. She had gone almost a month since the challenge of
her last case, that mess in BO-Media and Valiant said she would need
only Sunday.

Acting impulsively and excitedly, she returned to her email and
replied with a quick, "I'm in!"

⚥   ⚥   ⚥   ⚥   ⚥

At precisely 9:00 a.m. on Sunday Kelly entered the marble and
mahogany foyer of the estate, where a butler took her leather winter
coat. Not knowing what the day entailed, she had chosen a short-
jacketed black pants suit and a white blouse. She was admiring a

mounted weapon called the Singing Sword when she felt a tap on her shoulder. Turning abruptly, she looked at a familiar figure, who immediately hugged her.

"Dad," she said, "what are you doing here?"

"Same thing you are I imagine, my dear." He stroked the salt-and-pepper Van Dyke beard that had been getting saltier lately.

Recognizing his personal "The game's afoot" gesture, she agreed. "I have to admit I'm here as much for the intrigue as for charity." She omitted the boredom part. "Any idea what's going on?"

"One clue. We weren't the first to arrive. That honor goes to an old rival of yours." He pointed into the formal dining room with the stem of his unlit pipe.

"If it isn't Sherlock Holmes's great-great grand-daughter as I live and breathe," said a dark-haired woman in a white turtleneck sweater, black leather jacket and short heels moving toward Kelly.

"Ah," said Kelly, "the city's answer to Lois Lane. How are you, Marlowe?"

"Hoping the three of us have been asked over for something more than completing a bridge foursome, sweetie," replied the city's Pulitzer-Prize-winning crime reporter. She turned to Kelly's father. "So, Matt, got any hot leads for me?"

"The hottest thing I see is Marlowe Moore herself." The interrupting speaker was a tall, rawboned redhead whose tight-fitting houndstooth jacket revealed the obvious outline of a weapon beneath it. "Mike Kane," he said with a smile to Kelly. "I don't believe we've met."

"Mr. Kane is our city's newest private investigator," said her father. "Moved up here recently from Miami, though nobody knows why he'd leave the sunny south."

The redhead tugged on his diamond-studded earlobe. "Some people claim there's a woman to blame…"

"But," said Kelly, catching the Buffett allusion, "you know it's your own—"

"Damn fault," finished Marlowe. "I thought you said you were going to call me, Mike."

At that moment a loud trumpet sounded as though the first race was about to begin at the track. The butler tucked the long horn under his left armpit and announced, "Your host awaits you in the Grand Dining Hall."

The quartet entered a large room that towered three stories. It was paneled in oak, trimmed in medallions and covered with a variety of medieval weaponry from maces to pikes. At one end of the hall hung a round silver shield emblazoned with a red horse head.

"Greetings, noble friends," boomed a large man. With long hair and a white beard that reached his belt, he reminded Kelly of a hoary seer from the past or perhaps Gandalf from *Lord of the Rings*. "My name is Jonathan Valiant and I welcome you newcomers to my weekend league." He gestured toward a well-dressed man standing beside him. "First, I would like to introduce a permanent member of my League, Sir Ian Stock, formerly of MI-7, an organization so secret that he has not been able to mention it in his penny-dreadfuls for fear of being prosecuted under Her Majesty's Official Secrets Act. My friends, Ian has a sorrowful announcement."

"We would have another of our favorite members here," annunciated Stock in perfect King's English, "but Dame Ruby Elizabeth Marbles, known simply to her adoring mystery fans as Miss Marbles, met an unexpected and tragic end last weekend during a river cruise aboard *Cleopatra's Asp*. A cabin door at which she affixed her ear opened suddenly, knocking our dear friend into the crocodile-infested waters of the Nile."

"Alas," mourned Valiant, "we shall not look upon her like again. A moment of silence, please."

"Are we dreaming," whispered Kelly to her father, "or did we just step into a lost episode of *Masterpiece Theatre*?"

"Please be seated around the table," continued their host. "I have allotted one hour for our newcomers' brunch and after that begins our warm-up exercises."

"Had I known we were exercising," said Kelly to her father, who was seating her, "I'd have worn my best sweat suit."

"I don't know," answered Matt Locke. "For this gathering, a formal straitjacket might be most fitting."

"At this time," said the host, "I submit for your approval the nomination of two candidates to replace our dearly departed dame. Yes, I employed the plural, for perhaps it takes two to compensate for our loss. I offer you our fair city's version of Sherlock Holmes and Watson, Channel Four's investigative anchor Kelly Locke and her father, Chief of Detectives Matthew Locke."

A mild applause greeted the duo, who were forced to stand. "You were sent their credentials," continued Valiant, "so is there any dissension? Hearing none, I call the question."

"Aces," said Kane, sounding a little too much like Bogart for Kelly's comfort.

"Affirmative," echoed Stock in a military staccato.

"Far be it from me to prevent unanimity," groaned Marlowe.

Kelly found herself voted into the group before she knew what the group was.

"Let us eat," proclaimed Valiant amidst polite clapping.

Exactly half-an-hour into the feast, their host rose and struck a silver spoon to his water goblet. "As the Great Detective was wont to say in so many movies, but alas not in the canon, 'Perhaps you are wondering why I have called you together.'"

Kelly and the others nodded in the affirmative.

"Six decades ago my grandfather summoned the greatest investigators of his time together to form the powerful and secretive League of Mystery. Using prominent business models from brainstorming to criminology, he tasked those minds with finding solutions to the great unsolved crimes of the day. Do any among you know grandfather's inspiration?"

"Possibly Edgar Allan Poe's 'The Mystery of Marie Roget?'" suggested Kelly. "To solve the actual death of Mary Rogers, he devised a piece of fiction for his Dupin trilogy."

"Very good, Ms. Locke," said Valiant, taking a sip of wine from an ornate goblet. "You offer credence to your immense reputation."

Kelly didn't know whether to feel more embarrassed or praised.

"Now," continued their host, "here's something I don't believe even the very clever Ms. Locke suspected. My grandfather was a mystery writer who chose the *nom de plume* Julius Valiant, a last name continued to this day. Unfortunately the pulps and my grandfather expired at the same time. Even more unfortunately, at the time of his passing, Grandfather was serializing his *piece de resistance*, *Escape from Chillon Prison*, starring his most famous creation, Eurosleuth supreme, Simon Le Secret."

"I remember reading that as a child," exclaimed Matt Locke. "Except that it was published missing the last chapter."

"*Exactement!*" agreed Valiant. A tear formed in his eye that he clumsily knocked away. "Perhaps it is best that I let my recent bride finish my story."

The butler blew on his horn.

"Ten to one," whispered Kelly to her father, "the wife's name is Aleta."

"Ladies and gentlemen," announced Valiant, "I give you Aleta."

"That's an amazing deduction. How did you know?" said Matt Locke.

"Elementary, my dear Watson," replied Kelly with a smile. "An estate called Thule, the Singing Sword, a shield with red horse head, the fact that our host's grandfather chose the last name Valiant. Every Prince Valiant has his Aleta, Queen of the Misty Isles."

A tall woman in a flowing floor-length white robe and long jet-black hair entered the dining hall and stood directly beside the chair of Jonathan Valiant.

"What my husband has a difficult time saying is that he is dying of pancreatic cancer. Believe me, he has received the best treatment this world has to offer and recently has come to accept his. . . fate. During the past year we have grown closer than most couples who have been married decades and I have discovered my dear Jonathan possesses only two regrets. One is, of course, he has no family to carry on his proud name. And the second is that as a young boy, he was often read to by his grandfather, and yes, for you renown ratiocinators, one of those works was his Le Secret series. In fact, his grandfather used to read him the soon-to-be-published manuscripts—"

"And," completed Kelly, remembering her father's mentioning the famous unfinished last chapter, "he would like to know exactly how Le Secret performs his titular *Escape from Chillon Prison.*" What Kelly didn't say was she had that weird sense of having seen Aleta—whatever her real name was—somewhere else, but, of course, that was impossible.

"Perfect!" Aleta placed her hand tenderly on Valiant's shoulder and gave it a squeeze. "My husband is hesitant to admit he has perhaps a month to live, so with *tempus fugitting*, I have prevailed on him to call together the best minds of mystery for a personal reason, to provide him a solution to a puzzle that has dogged him for half a century."

"Perhaps not Grandfather's precise solution," chimed in Valiant, "because there are no lost manuscripts to be unearthed in time, but a solution. You see, Aleta is right. Before I meet my. . . fate, I simply must know how my boyhood hero could have escaped the greatest of locked rooms, *Cachat Numbero Un* in Chillon Castle. I've always had an idea as to the solution, but I need affirmation. And what better group from whom to get it?"

The modern-day League of Mystery gave the dying man a standing ovation.

"Thank you, my friends, for agreeing to help an old man. And Ms. Locke, it seems that my dear Aleta was correct in insisting I invite you to take Miss Marbles's place at the table—and even bring your well-known father to join our merry company."

Valiant cleared his throat. "Now there is something I must show you. Please leave your cellphones on the side table and follow me." He led them down a paneled hallway into a large room whose walls were lined with volume-filled bookcases. "And what does every child want a room such as this one to contain?"

"A nanny to read to him?" ventured Stock.

Valiant ignored the response. "Grandfather's old friend Hal Foster, who created Prince Valiant, once explained to him why he was going to stop illustrating the Tarzan comic strip with 'I need one of my own.' Well, I need a secret panel of my own."

Pulling on a brass sconce, their host smiled as a heavy wooden panel swung open to reveal a secret passage. "*Voila*, as Le Secret would often say."

Valiant led them down steps and along a narrow rock-lined corridor. When he came to a large metal door he punched in an entrance code and the door swung open. "*Apres vous, mes amis.*"

One by one the modern-day League of Mystery filed into a cavernous room that resembled an old-time dungeon. Then suddenly the door slammed behind them and they were left in pure darkness.

The usually ultra-composed Marlowe Moore let out a piercing yell.

"Why are skirts so prone to screaming?" said Mike Kane in the pitch black.

"It's a cultural thing," pronounced Stock. "English women gasp."

"Let there be light," said Matt Locke, using the lighter usually reserved for his pipe.

"Is this some kind of initiation rite?" said Kelly.

Suddenly a giant monitor above them flashed on and a picture of Valiant and Aleta appeared. "A good question, Ms. Locke," said Valiant, "but I have constructed an exact down-to-the-last-detail replica of *Cachat Numero Un* as described in my grandfather's final novel, though I did refrain from pumping in the foul gas that so unsettled Le Secret."

"So," said Marlowe, "as a thank-you for the companionship we've given you in the past, you are kidnapping us?"

"Nonsense," said Valiant. "I went to great expense to provide you not with a theoretical, but a real problem and Aleta thought placing you inside offered an extra incentive to secure the solution swiftly."

"I really hate to bring the matter up in mixed company," said Stock, "but we all have certain needs…"

"I am not a monster," protested Valiant. "In fact, I have made two alterations to Grandfather's description. In the right corner is a fake boulder behind which you will find men's and women's—I believe, Ian, you call them—loos. In the left corner sits a similar boulder, behind which is an ample supply of food and drink."

Marlowe pulled out her cellphone that she failed to leave on the library's side table. "I'm not getting any bars."

"Six decades ago, my dear," said Valiant, "the only bars in here were those at the top that prevented prisoners from escaping. Should there be a medical emergency, let me know by simply shouting. My personal physician is currently residing in my guest cottage. Oh, should you require them, I have left half a dozen cots in your room. Sorry, no night lights. One last thing. The room contains the only exit I believe my grandfather could have 'secreted' away. Please prove me correct."

With that the screen went black and sconces on the walls flickered on, providing a dim but sufficient light.

"Now let's get this straight," boomed Matt Locke in his best Chief of Detectives' take-charge voice. "The three of you are members of some wacky club that Valiant's organized so he has someone to play mystery games with."

"You've got that right," said Kane. "The old man gets his jollies watching us argue over what method for crime-solving works best."

Ian Stock straightened his boarding school tie. "Our host reveled in all sorts of mysteries from diamond thefts to murder and seeing which of us could come up with the most plausible solution."

"Sort of a cut-throat game of Clue," interjected Kelly.

"Hadn't thought of it exactly that way," said Marlowe, "but, yes, it was a competition. Hardboiled, thriller, procedural… and even dying clue."

"Alas," bemoaned Stock, "when we lost our dear Marbles, I suppose the blighter selected you as a disciple of Mr. Holmes to take her place."

Recalling that Valiant said the choice was actually his wife's, Kelly wondered that perhaps Aleta desired to keep the gender balance intact.

"Enough chit-chat, ladies," bellowed Kane. "Let's figure out this puzzle and get the hell outta here—I've got a hot date planned for tonight."

"What a unique way to describe a TV dinner and Jimmy Cagney marathon," purred Marlowe.

Kane shot a look at the crime reporter that bordered on a crime itself.

Kelly turned to Matt Locke. "Dad, you're the expert when it comes to Valiant the elder and the Le Secret series. Do you remember what happened in that last book?"

Matt Locke pulled his pipe from his jacket and twirled it between his right thumb and index finger. "As I recall, Le Secret was closing in on his arch-nemesis, Emile L'Etoile, when the dastardly mathematician turned smuggler of historic artifacts tricked him into the Chillon

Castle dungeon and began piping in a deadly gas. L'Etoile left our hero a message informing him that he had but one hour to figure out an escape and save his life."

Kelly chuckled. "An interesting twist on the classic locked-room mystery. Le Secret's problem was *getting out* of the room."

"I fear, my good woman," said Stock, "our only danger is in boring each other to death, but I have a flight to London scheduled for 6:00 this evening, so in the immortal last words of Sartre's *No Exit*, 'Let's get on with it.'"

"How appropriate," said Marlowe, "the same play that tells us, 'Hell is other people.'"

"And what about my hot date?" nagged Kane.

"Get real, dude," said Marlowe, sarcasm dripping from her lips like wax from a candle. "The only women in your life charge for dates or come with instruction on how to inflate. I, on the other hand, am scheduled to receive yet another journalistic award at the Chamber banquet tonight. If I'm not there, they're liable to present it to that slut from *The Inquirer* who's more interested in exposing her body than corruption."

"Then," said Kelly's father, "I suggest we put our heads together and figure a way out. I must warn you, though, since Julius Valiant's death writers and mystery fans around the globe have put forth possible methods of escape, but all have been found lacking."

Kane moved toward the door. "I say we just batter our way out. I see some iron racks we can use as rams."

"Did you notice the thickness of the door as we came in?" said Matt Locke. "You'd need a bulldozer to push it open."

"And there are no other doors or windows," said Marlowe.

Stock was strutting around the room, lifting tapestries and peering behind the few pictures on the sparsely decorated walls. As he tugged at a table in the corner, he exploded. "Balderdash! No trap doors or secret passages that I can discern. Oh, how I miss my beloved Miss Marbles."

Kelly walked toward the door. "Dad, didn't you tell me that L'Etoile was, like our old friend Moriarty, a mathematician at heart?"

"That's right," agreed Kelly's father. "Every time Le Secret had a run in with him, the case somehow turned on numbers."

Kelly studied the locked steel door. For the first time, she noticed that, unlike most dungeon doors, there was no keyhole. Instead, a combination dial made the door seem like it belonged on a 19th-Century safe. "If I don't miss my guess, the way out of here involves cracking the combination of this lock."

Kelly's father bent over for a clearer look at the 1–100 dial. "You may be right, Kelly. Figuring a number sequence would be in keeping with previous Le Secret vs. L'Etoile confrontations."

"That's just great," interrupted Marlowe. "Give me a real-life crime to solve, not some theoretical exercise in mathematical permutations."

"We're bloody detectives, love," blurted out Stock, "not sandpaper-fingered safe-crackers. The only thing I can see in our futures is my bloody plane departing without me."

Kane kicked the door and let out a scream of pain. "And my date—"

"Give it a rest, Mike," begged Marlowe. "You can't punch your way out of every case."

"Let's not panic," said Kelly, mindful of her own need to get out of the room in time to make the trial. "Valiant said that he always had an idea about the unprinted solution, so we might conclude it involves a combination of numbers somehow meaningful to him and/or his grandfather."

"I agree," said Matt Locke, "but Valiant is so private, what numbers special to him could we possibly know?"

"The value of his personal wealth?" suggested Marlowe.

"Not relevant to his grandfather," said Kelly.

"Then," said Marlowe, "could the numbers have something to do with L'Etoile's or Le Secret's life?"

"Even if Valiant believes his grandfather had such numbers in mind," said Kelly, "he wouldn't know what they could have been."

"Nobody knows Valiant's birthdate or even the date of his marriage to Aleta," said Stock. "I feel like we're forever trapped on a roundabout."

"Aha," said Matt Locke. "What if Valiant set the lock for the date on which his grandfather died?"

"Ingenious, mate," said the suddenly renewed Englishman. "How appropriate and an homage to his grandfather's genius. Just as L'Etoile would have set the combination to correspond to Le Secret's day of death, so Valiant has set our lock to fit the day both Julius Valiant and Le Secret died."

"Dad," said Kelly, "this is important. Do you remember the date?"

"Any self-respecting law enforcement official would." Matt Locke reached for the dial. "March 11, 1927, same date as the first armored car robbery in this country. 3-11-27." He turned the dial left, then right, then left. Grabbing the massive handle, he pulled down... nothing.

"Rot," said Stock. "Let me try. Right 3… left 11… right 27." Still nothing.

"I told you," said Marlowe, assuming the role of team pessimist. "We might as well wait till the old bugger lets us out. Goodbye prime rib and peer adulation."

"Just a second," interrupted Kelly. "Secret Agent Man, I can't believe you missed it, what with your love of all things European."

"What are you getting at, sister?" said Kane.

"The combination of numbers, gumshoe," shot back Kelly. "In the States we give the month, then day, then year when referring to a date. Europeans, like the military, always provide the day first, then the month, then the year. Dad, try 11-3-27."

Matt Locke spun the dial through the combination, then pulled on the handle. With a groan the massive door opened.

✗   ✗   ✗   ✗   ✗

Just as quickly the monitor flickered on and Valiant, shaking his head, exclaimed, "Aleta bet me it would take you days, so I'm impressed… no, make that astonished."

Mike Kane pointed his trigger finger toward the screen. "Got you, big guy! You didn't really think you could outwit a collection of deep thinkers like us, did you?"

"Mr. Kane," said Valiant, "don't forget I've been watching you since locking the door and from my vantage point I'd have to say the League of Mystery ought to thank its lucky stars Aleta had me invite the Lockes to join us."

"You're too kind," said Kelly, "but if you don't mind, I have to be going. I have some last minute prep for an important appointment early in the morning. Just send the check to the Wounded Warriors Project," she added, thinking of her brother Miles.

"And I have a plane to catch," said Stock, "though not as comfortable since they grounded the SST."

"And I have something even more important," Marlowe reminded, "a banquet and an award."

"What about my assignment?" protested Kane.

"I think you mean assignation, old man," said Stock.

As the group emerged from the passageway into the library, they were greeted by their host and his wife.

"I fear," Valiant said, "I must prevail on your patience for a bit longer. "To celebrate your success, Aleta has been supervising Chef Reynard in the preparation of a sumptuous dinner to be served at precisely 8:00 and she will not hear of your departing."

Kane bristled. "We all have places to go. We played your little game by your little rules—now just give us our checks and we'll be gone."

"You were promised payment at the end of the process," Valiant reminded them, "and until dinner ends we have not concluded our business. Leave now and you forfeit any recompense."

The group exchanged glances.

"Well," said Marlowe, "I'm already going to have to buy a trophy case to house all my awards and I doubt the chef's meal will be overcooked."

"Flights are like excuses from a woman," said Stock. "There's always another one."

Hey," said Kane, not to be one-upped, "dames are like streetcars… if you know what I mean."

Putting the misogyny behind her, Kelly crossed over to the side table and retrieved her iPhone.

"Who are you calling?" asked her father.

"Nobody," said Kelly. "This whole situation's got me thinking and I want to check out a few things I have stored on my computer at home."

"What could Valiant's little game have to do with anything you've been working on?" questioned Matt Locke.

"Just give me a minute and I'll let you know," Kelly said, concentrating on the small screen.

As the group was starting to filter out of the library, Kelly approached Aleta Valiant. "I want to thank you for a delightful diversion. By the way, was it your husband who insisted on your changing your name to Aleta?"

Aleta tittered. "I'll have to plead guilty. I so wanted to enter into his juvenile fantasy of becoming Prince Valiant."

"Aleta is such a prettier name than Maria, anyway," added Kelly.

Aleta Valiant's perfectly tanned face suddenly turned the color of winter snow. "What do you mean… Maria?"

The others stopped and turned toward the two women.

"Maria," said Kelly, "as in Maria Constantine, sister of Dante Constantine, infamous international criminal—and if I don't miss my guess, worse."

"Wait just a minute, Ms. Locke," interrupted Valiant, who took his wife's hand. "You have no right to accept our hospitality and then engage in slander."

Matt Locke looked directly into Valiant's face. "Sir, I assure you that if my daughter makes a claim, it is supported by solid evidence."

"Thanks, Dad," said Kelly. "You know I've been prepping for the Mary Sutherland trial for the last week. The poor woman has been charged with the theft of over half a million in bearer bonds from her investment firm. Although Dante Constantine's fingerprints were found at the scene, he had what seemed an air-tight alibi."

"Yes," said Matt Locke, "I had my best men on that case from the onset."

"Well, as you know," said Kelly, "Carpenter and Apostel Investments has its office right down the street from Channel 4. As luck would have it, I was walking to dinner on the night of the theft and I snapped some pictures of the Noel Building because we were doing a story on art deco architecture. I called Mary Sutherland's attorney last week because when I looked carefully at my pictures, guess what I noticed?"

"What?" ventured her father.

"Dante Constantine coming out of the Noel Building. Bye, bye, alibi. My pictures and I will exonerate Mary tomorrow and implicate Constantine."

"What does all this have to do with my wife?" asked Valiant.

"Ever since I first saw your wife this afternoon, I've had a strange feeling I'd seen her before, but I couldn't quite pin it down till I checked a photo file I have in my computer at home." Kelly punched a few buttons on her iPhone. "Anybody look familiar?"

The Chief of Detectives studied the picture. "That's Mrs. Valiant in the picture... and that man with her—"

"Is Dante Constantine," Kelly said, retrieving her iPhone. "That picture was taken a couple of years ago by a paparazzo at the Constantine villa in San Moritz. Check out the accompanying news story that identifies the woman as Maria Constantine, sister of Dante."

Aleta Valiant's face grew even paler, while during the confrontation the usually gregarious members of the League stood silent.

Still looking directly at their hostess, Kelly continued. "Keeping your brother free meant keeping me from testifying. We may not be able to prove that Dante intended to kill dear Miss Marbles, but I'll bet security video on *Cleopatra's Asp* will reveal he was on the boat at the time of her death. He had to keep her away so his sister could convince a husband who adores her to invite me as a replacement to participate in a game I'm sure she encouraged him in creating."

"I built the dungeon years ago to help me solve Le Secret's last case, but the day's event was Aleta's... my wife's," admitted Valiant.

"But why was I invited?" said Matt Locke.

"Because Maria knew that if I didn't show up for the trial, you'd come looking for me... a complication she didn't need."

"So if Aleta, I mean Maria, were successful," said the Chief of Detectives, "Mary Sutherland would be convicted on circumstantial evidence and this unscrupulous woman and her brother continue their life of larceny."

"I'm beginning to think that plan was only a small strategy in a larger battle," said Kelly. "You remember Maria, a/k/a Aleta, saying her recent husband has no heir to his immense fortune… well, none but her."

Jonathan Valiant released his wife's hand. "How could I have been so foolish! I've managed the lives and money of so many, but couldn't direct my own."

At that moment Mike Kane strolled in from the dining hall, a large turkey drumstick in his right mitt. "Don't know what you folks are jabbering about, but I'm starved. Can we just eat?"

Kelly snatched the drumstick from his hand.

"Hey," said the private investigator, "I know it's a little impolite to start the meal early, but—"

"It's liable to also be a little poisoned or at least contain something stronger than tryptophan to make us sleep. I'm convinced that this dinner Valiant insisted on us partaking of, one that Maria helped Chef Reynard prepare, was her back-up plan if we managed to figure out the puzzle. We were all going to take if not the big sleep, the little sleep."

"A little one, I promise," sobbed the woman.

Matt Locke was on his cell phone immediately calling for back-up. At the very least, Kelly knew, Maria would be charged as an accessory after the fact… at the worst, murder.

"Dad," said Kelly, when her father hung up, "doesn't this affair remind you of one of your favorite Holmes stories?"

The Chief of Detectives tucked his cell in his coat pocket. "Of course. 'The Red-Headed League.'"

"Look at the parallels," Kelly began. "The crime hinges on misdirection. Everybody must pay attention to the red herring while the real crime is occurring elsewhere. Maria's instigation of our solving her husband's life-long mystery and even the ensuing meal were meant to keep us occupied—make that, trapped—until the trial was over."

"Well," said Marlowe, "this beats rubber chicken and un-needed hardware any day."

"You're aces with me, doll," said Kane to Kelly while leering at the reporter.

"MI-7 has nothing on your cleverness, my dear," agreed Stock. "Cheerio."

Matt Locke chuckled. "Good thing we had all that support from the League."

Kelly looked at the threesome, the self-proclaimed Masters of Mystery as they hung their heads. "Perhaps they should take a cue from Maria and change their names… perhaps to something like The Red-Faced League."

✗

"Hal Charles" is the nom de plume Fred Dannay (one-half of Ellery Queen) gave to the writing team of Hal Blythe and Charlie Sweet. Retired professors of English at Eastern Kentucky University, they are well-versed in mysteries, having written for *Ellery Queen Mystery Magazine* and being the final ghost of Brett Halliday (Mike Shayne). They have published seven stories in the Kelly Locke series as well as nine novels.

SUCH GOOD FRIENDS

by Dianne Neral Ell

The miles spun beneath her wheels as Devon January headed south into the Florida Keys toward the city of Marathon. It was a perfect September day. The traffic along the Overseas Highway was scattered and the blue-green waters on both sides of the two-lane road glinted gold under the rays of the late morning sun.

Meeting her in Marathon was a Coast Guard officer willing to talk about the investigation into the death of her long-time friend Barbra Symonds It was early August two years ago when the world-class artist disappeared from her forty-two foot boat the *Sky Dragon* anchored just off the Marathon coastline. Barbra's disappearance caused a media frenzy, then a week later when her body washed ashore and no signs of foul play were evident, everyone moved on, leaving the police to grapple with their problem. At that time, Devon was in Baghdad covering the Middle East war for Global Media Inc. Too far away to be of any help, all she could do was follow the story and express her anger and disappointment when the investigation didn't take a more vigorous route. It stalled for lack of clues, then interest withered and died until it became just another unsolved death.

Now having returned to Miami, finished with the Middle East and ducking bullets from insurgents, she was ready to take on "The Last Days of Barbra Symonds," as she was calling her assignment. Time to uncover what happened to her childhood friend.

Barb Symonds wasn't an ordinary artist. Her last bird sculpture, the Phoenix, was for the palace in Beirut. Other works could be seen in the White House, the Louvre and New York's Museum of Modern Art. Her gallery Symonds Design and Art Restoration was still in business, located in the design section of Miami. And the home she used for much of her artistry was here in the town of Key Colony, connected to Marathon by a one-way in one-way out causeway.

To get started, Devon needed to interview the local law enforcement agencies. Topping her list was the Coast Guard who guided the original investigation. The agent in charge had a territory to cover and when he called and offered to talk to her that Tuesday morning Devon jumped at the chance.

She made the two-hour journey from Miami, arriving ten minutes early at the marina. Before leaving the car, she checked her makeup and re-pinned her shoulder-length blond hair into a knot at the base of her neck.

Agent Michael Tureau welcomed her and immediately ushered her aboard a waiting Coast Guard vessel. "Our destination is the area where Barb Symonds anchored the *Sky Dragon* for those last three days. Nothing like returning to the scene of the crime to get a perspective." He steered the boat toward the open sea. His easy manner made Devon feel at ease. He looked at her, then back at the panel that showed their location.

"You're the Devon January who writes for *NewsWeekly*?"

"Yes, not hardly anyone knows my name." She laughed. "How do you?"

"I like your writing and follow your adventures. You report news, not interpret it. which is refreshing. So you're home now and Barb Symonds is your next assignment. How'd you draw that?"

"Friends since eighth grade…"

"Oh. Very sorry. Strange case."

"In what way?"

"We're almost there." Within a minute he slowed, then stopped, putting the engine into idle.

Devon looked around. "Barb wrote that she anchored here frequently for inspiration."

They were in a kind of protected area. The towns of Key Colony and Marathon occupied the western shore with businesses and homes extending as far north as the eye could see. To the south forming a type of barrier was Sombrero Beach and then Boot Key. Otherwise it was the open sea. And on this day the water was smooth like ice.

She took out her camera and began to take photos. Her attention was on the houses that lined the shore.

"Anyone with a really good camera could have had a photo of the *Sky Dragon* while it was out here. As well as any other boats. I went aboard the *Sky Dragon* a few days ago. There isn't any way she accidentally went overboard. Even if she tried to jump, she'd have a hard time getting footing and clearing the walkways that stick out from the sides. So what happened to Barb?"

"Monday she came out here and anchored. Tuesday, one of the locals Ray Bradshaw brought her pizza for lunch. Wednesday was the storm. Thursday, when Ray didn't hear from her, he went out and found the boat deserted and called Chief McKinsey. The investigating officers from all three branches initially believed that she went overboard during the storm. When it became apparent that didn't happen, they worked on theory number two. And that was an abduction."

"So they did look at something else? Was that in the report?"

"Don't know. The problem was that there was no evidence to support it. An abduction would have required another boat. There were boats out here, but no one saw anything suspicious. There was also nothing on board the *Sky Dragon* that indicated a fight, a struggle. The interior was neat, clean, all her artist supplies were in order. It didn't even appear she had been working on anything. Monroe County Sheriff Martin Edwards has the photos. So that theory was dropped after a while and nothing else took its place. The case is open, waiting for you to solve it."

"Outside of Bradshaw, did anyone else from the town visit her?" she asked.

"Not that we know of."

"What's your theory? Were you on the case two years ago?'

"No. I've been in this position about six months. I do believe she left the *Sky Dragon* via a second boat. I've reviewed all the data. Did second interviews of locals. Next stop is family and friends. But maybe you'll have some insight I don't."

She finished her picture taking. "Where does Ray Bradshaw live?"

"One of those houses." He pointed across the water to homes lining the shoreline. "Key Colony police have his address." He started up the engine and headed back to the marina.

Once they reached the dock, he handed her his business card. "Any other questions?"

"I can save you some time," she said, handing him her business card. She wrote a different email address on the back. "That's my personal. The other is business."

"I was hoping you'd have something."

"I believe there was a second boat and my guess is that Barb went on board late afternoon to evening of the eighth. One of the Symonds Group board members has a boat the size of hers. His name is John Ryder and the boat is the *Oh-Twenty-Seven*. That was his number when he played for the Dolphins. What happened to my friend may very well be business-related."

"John Ryder," he repeated and made a note.

"I don't know what might have been going on two years ago, but I'm sure there's a way to find out," she said. "Maybe it was a meeting. Maybe there were papers to sign. Maybe they were just getting together."

"But, remember, whatever transpired ended up in her death," he said. "Was John Ryder capable of that?"

"Maybe what happened was an accident."

"It wasn't. Doesn't have that feel. Sorry. And if it was, he would have called for help rather than allowing her to drown," Tureau said.

After a long thoughtful sigh, she said, "John's capable."

"All right. I'm on it. I'll go in that direction and see what turns up. Also, you'll find the Chief here pretty helpful. He was here when she disappeared. Martin Edwards from Monroe wasn't. He came in a few months later. He's in charge of major crimes and Barb's death qualified as that. But there's something else going on with him. Just be careful."

"What's Bradshaw's game?"

"He was something in law enforcement a ways back. But he says his passion is photography. It's entirely possible that he has photos of that Tuesday. I don't think he was ever asked."

"Thanks. Good to know. When you leave here where do you go?"

"Boca Chica. Nice ride."

Devon thanked him for his help.

"I'll be back to you as soon as I can," he said.

✗　✗　✗　✗　✗

She parked her car in the garage and went upstairs to her fifth-floor corner apartment that overlooked Brickell Avenue and Biscayne Bay beyond. On her journey back to Miami, she thought about the meeting. It was apparent that Barb's death was no longer the accidental swept- overboard drama she imagined. Murder was much more tragic than dramatic. But now she needed to shift gears. Buried in Barb's demise was some type of corporate intrigue. And that changed everything.

She thought she could go this alone. But now she needed her dad's help and maybe even that of her good friend Al Bek who was heading up a new museum on South Beach.

She called him first.

"Are you back or did you stay down there?" he asked in his British accent.

"Drove back. The officer was helpful. Says Barb's death was not an accident. That a second boat was involved. And that brings me to the Symonds Group. Have you had any contact with them?"

"Yes. With Justin. He's helping me out with pieces for the new wing of the museum and I'm trying to talk him into giving me first option on the three Barbra birds that are in inventory."

"Inventory?" Sitting at the kitchen table, Devon scribbled the word on a notepad. "I didn't know there was an inventory on the birds."

"Go to the gallery. They're displayed."

"I thought those were Chantal Lee's."

"Maybe I'm wrong, but they were labeled Barbra Symonds. Maybe the label was wrong."

"Or I'm thinking of different birds." Devon backed off knowing the gallery was on her list of things to do. "I need your help. From around the time that Barb died, did you ever hear of any problems at Symonds? With the group? With any of their artists? I don't know what I'm looking for. Just something out of place."

"Not off hand. Let me see what I can come up with. Going to Martha Sellers reception at the Art Museum tonight? I'll pick you up at seven. Barb's last bird is on exhibit."

"I forgot. See you then."

The next call was to her dad Don January, head counsel for Global Media.

"I'm back," she said as he answered. "Good interview. More questions than answers. We need to talk. The investigating officer believes Barb was murdered."

"Goodness. That can't be. How could the company exist without her? Any chance he's wrong?"

"I'm going to look into it. Talked to Al. He's working with Justin to find pieces for his new wing. He said there's three birds in inventory."

"There aren't. The glass birds displayed at the gallery are Chantal's, not Barb's. I've been through this with Martha Sellers. Chantal Lee is an excellent artist. Almost better than Barb is—was—in many areas."

"How do you prove they're not Barb's?"

"Easiest way is materials. Barb used a different composition than Chantal. You should know that. Are you going to Martha's reception tonight? She's displaying for Symonds Gallery the last bird Barb did. I've seen it. Exquisite. Wing span of about two feet."

"Al's picking me up at seven. See you there or do you want to ride with us?"

"I'll think about it."

✗ ✗ ✗ ✗ ✗

The reception was well-attended and her dad was right about the bird. A hawk. Wing span of over two feet, poised ready to take flight with its eyes on a distant horizon. Lighting helped to give it an eerie quality, but it was the incredible detail with glass that sent Barb to the top of the art world.

Justin Walker was there, along with Morgan Price, Barb's cousin and a trial attorney. She wondered if they were on board John's boat the night Barb died.

"I'm working on a story about Barb for one of Global's magazines," she said to both of them. "I'll need your help in identifying all of the birds. I'd like to include photos of them as well as the gallery."

"I'm there tomorrow," Justin said. "Is that too soon?"

"That's good. I need to go to the Keys sometime later to talk to the police. Barb's death is not going to go away, so it needs to be handled delicately."

"They're finished with the investigation, aren't they?" Morgan asked, her voice becoming sharp.

"No. Until they know what happened to her it's an open case. They have a theory about a second boat that they're working on." For a moment, she saw something flicker in Justin's eyes. But it was the look he and Morgan exchanged that told her she was on the right track. "I'll see you tomorrow. I'll be there about ten-thirty."

⚡ ⚡ ⚡ ⚡ ⚡

The next morning the phone rang at eight. It was Mike Tureau from the Coast Guard.

"Thank you for the photo of John Ryder's boat."

"Got it from my dad last night at dinner."

"I turned it into our division chief. He was happy, since two years at a dead end wasn't making him look good. As it turned out, another section has Ryder under surveillance. They suspect he's involved in some type of smuggling operation, but haven't anything solid yet. So maybe linking him to Barbra Symonds's death will turn up something no one anticipated. But that's not why I called. John Ryder's name stuck in my mind, so I called a friend who works in the legal area. He came up with *The State of Florida versus Barbra Symonds*. Did you know that the major crimes unit of the U.S. Attorney's office was after her two years back for art and artifact fraud and smuggling?"

"What? That can't be. Maybe their information isn't right?"

"A possibility, but I don't think so. But it's her defense attorney who was the biggest surprise. Martin Edwards. He was brought in by John Ryder. The case was headed for the grand jury. A few days before, the prosecuting attorney was killed. A week after that Barb Symonds died. And the case died with it."

"This is unbelievable."

"There was a rumor that Barb may have been involved in the prosecutor's murder."

"Oh." She sighed. "The webs we weave. We were such good friends. How did I miss the change?"

"If you're heading to Marathon, beware of Martin Edwards."

The afternoon vanished as Devon waited for the report from the U.S. Attorney's office. Finally, at five and ready to leave regardless, the fax came in. She left with a copy and messaged her dad that she was going home, packing and heading to Marathon. She'd be there before dark. Nothing to worry about.

It was after six when she entered the Turnpike going south toward Florida City. The sun like an uncooked pancake hung low in the sky. Sunset was just two hours away.

She didn't begin to feel the chill of her decision until she passed Tavernier—a half hour south of Key Largo. By this time local traffic as well as long distance to Miami dissipated. Keeping Martin Edwards in mind, she put her gun on the seat beside her. Plantation Key was next and just south of that was Islamorada. Beyond, there was nothing but small wisps of land supporting the two-lane highway that ran over it. Nothing for thirty miles except the road and water on both sides. And growing darkness.

The miles passed. With Islamorada now behind her, there was nothing ahead but long stretches of bridges. She turned off the radio to concentrate on her driving. It anyone was going to attack her, it would be in this stretch. It was just after eight o'clock, but the sun was already racing to slide beyond the horizon. Only a purple sky with bands of gold remained. An occasional car passed in the opposite direction, but other than that she was pretty much alone.

When the sign for Duck Key finally appeared, the tension eased from her shoulders. Just a few more miles.

Her relaxing came a little too soon. It was just a few yards south of the Duck Key entrance when she felt a bang against the back of the driver side. It pushed her car to the right, nearly making her lose control. This was a two-lane highway with low guardrails and a short stretch of rocks that descended to the Gulf of Mexico. She looked through the mirrors, but couldn't see anything. She took firm hold of the steering wheel and pressed down on the gas pedal as a plan formed. The Dolphin Research Center would be coming up on the right and shortly she'd be on Vaca Key, the northern end of Marathon.

With an eye on the side-view mirror, she saw the black car come up along the driver side. She could make out a man in the passenger seat. He was wearing a baseball cap and pointing a gun. The car was getting ready to slam hers again. If hit, she could go through the guardrails, but she braced herself and timed the attack. At the precise moment, as the car swung toward hers, Devon hit the brakes. The other car with the momentum to continue right, passed her and kept veering toward the water. It tried to stop, but too late as it hit the guard rail and rolled down the rocks. It was nose deep in the Gulf when it came to a stop. Devon looked over the side. When no one appeared to be hurt she got out of there.

Twenty minutes later, she checked into the Marathon Inn. She phoned her dad. It was Thursday. The restaurant was open. She grabbed dinner and took it to her room, turned on the TV and fell asleep.

She didn't wake until the hotel phone rang. It was morning. A deep voice with a southern drawl introduced himself as Chief Garrett McKinsey of the Key Colony Police.

"I was calling to invite you to breakfast. Nice little place near Sombrero Beach."

"If you're driving, I can be ready in twenty minutes. Thank you for calling me back," she said.

"All in the name of justice," he replied.

The sheriff was right about the restaurant being a nice place. Rustic, great view of the water and an interesting menu. They talked a little about her investigation, then he said:

"Last night, a car ended up in the Gulf just north of the Dolphin Research Center. You wouldn't know anything about that, would you?"

As Devon thought about how to answer, he said, "I told them it was that crazy reporter just back from the Middle East who forgot how to drive in the States."

"You really told them that." Devon laughed.

"How'd you do it? Those were two mean guys."

"Learned defensive driving in the Army. Came in handy over the years."

"Well, someone's out to get you. Who knew you were coming down last night?"

"Only my dad. I planned on leaving this morning, then changed my mind at the last minute."

"Someone back home is following you. But after last night," he laughed, "maybe not."

The Chief packed too many pounds into his uniform, but probably most of it was muscle. He moved quickly and easily. Tanned, dark eyes and brown hair with a lot of gray. Someone she wanted on her side, Devon thought.

Within a few minutes, the waitress placed plates of eggs, biscuits and several slices of ham and roasted potatoes in front of each of them. The sheriff dug right in.

"Ray Bradshaw was the first on board that Thursday morning. Did you have a problem with that?" she asked.

"You mean, could he have taken anything, changed things around and totally messed up the case? Yes, he could have and probably did. Can't prove it, though. He's not one of our outstanding citizens, but he comes in handy as you'll find. Have you been out to where she anchored?"

"Yesterday. With Mike Tureau from the Coast Guard. I was also on board the *Sky Dragon* a few days ago. The boat is innocent."

He smiled. "The second boat theory?" He looked at her expectantly as he buttered a biscuit.

"It's the only thing that makes sense."

"The Coast Guard proposed that. But it was the heavy guns from Monroe County that shot it down. They may have solved the case if it hadn't been for Martin Edwards."

"I've been told to be aware. I'm meeting with him later."

"If you're looking for information in the days before she disappeared, poke around. Try the waterfront in Key Colony. Especially the marina. If there was a second boat, it might have come in for fuel."

They finished breakfast, the plates were cleared, Devon took the check and the sheriff pulled a business card from his wallet. He wrote a cell number on it.

"You may need this before it's all over. Call. Doesn't matter what the time is."

⚓   ⚓   ⚓   ⚓   ⚓

Her appointment with Martin Edwards was scheduled for the afternoon. He was coming up from Key West. It was nearly four o'clock when she finally sat down across from him in a conference room in the county office building not far from the hotel.

He didn't fit the role of sheriff. But he did look like someone who could have been defending Barb Symonds against the U.S. Attorney's office. He was slick. He had dark hair and if it was turning gray, he made sure it didn't. He was somewhere maybe late forties and wasn't as friendly as the Chief.

He showed her the official crime scene photos. There wasn't much. Her photos of the *Sky Dragon* were better, but she asked for copies of the boat's interior. Martin Edwards wasn't willing to spend time with her. He kept looking at his watch. Then he stood, calling the meeting to an end, but Devon wasn't finished.

"What about that Tuesday? Any photos from that day?"

"We weren't on the scene until Thursday. Try Ray Bradshaw."

"I was thinking of satellite photos. NOAA, Boca Chica."

"What are you looking for?"

"The second boat. There was one."

Devon tried to make it sound casual, but she knew she had him. There was a second boat and he knew about it. Was he on it the night Barb died? He was a friend of John Ryder's.

Outside she watched him walk to his car, imagining the ice that ran through his veins.

✗   ✗   ✗   ✗   ✗

It was nearly six when she arrived at Ray Bradshaw's house. Two-story stucco. It was on the water and from the side of the house, she could see a dock that extended out with a power boat anchored at the end. She caught Bradshaw as he was leaving his house.

"Mr. Bradshaw." Devon introduced herself. They shook hands as she quickly explained what she was looking for.

He looked at the time. "I can give you ten minutes. I hope that's enough."

Bradshaw looked to be in his late fifties. Skin tanned by hours spent fishing. Or whatever he used his boat for. He had a face that was expressionless but lined by time.

"You said you were looking for photos before the storm."

"I'm looking for Monday and Tuesday. The Chief at Key Colony thought you could help."

He seemed on edge as they went into the house, then walked out to his backyard which was all deck with pots of flowers and no grass.

"From here you can see where Barb Symonds boat was anchored. Did you get out there?"

"Yes." Then Devon looked to her left. She stared for a moment at a house across the bay. "That's Key Colony." She said surprised, "You can see Barb Symonds property."

"Yeah. So what are you looking for?"

"On that Monday and Tuesday, were there other boats out there besides Barb's?"

"There's always boats out there. This is what I've got." He led her inside and opened a file drawer, taking out an orange file folder. It was filled with black and white photos. Devon browsed through them, then stopped. "Here's something. The same power boat Monday and Tuesday, but on Tuesday it looks like it could have gotten near the *Sky Dragon*."

Bradshaw looked over her shoulder. "Could have or maybe it's just the angle."

"Ah, true. But it could be a clue." It was John Ryder's. She was positive.

"Recognize it?" he asked.

She wasn't about to give him anything. "No. But if it was here for at least a day, someone at the marina should know something about it."

They both stared at the larger than forty-foot boat that hauled itself nearly alongside the *Sky Dragon*. The time stamp indicated early evening Tuesday at 6:34 p.m.

"Do you mind if I take a photo of it?"

"Whatever. If he needed fuel, he would have stopped at the marina. But it's been two years. No telling what people remember."

"Do you have any satellite photos? From NOAA, Boca Chica."

"No. Let me make a few calls. It's possible to get lucky, now that we have a day and time."

Ray disappeared into another room. He returned five minutes later. "My friend at Boca Chica says NOAA would have them. He gave me the name of their contact person. I called. They'll have something tomorrow late afternoon. We'll have to drive down there or you can meet me there. It's on Big Pine Key. Not far."

"Thank you. I know this is rude," Devon said, "but do you have binoculars? I'd like to get a look at Barb Symonds's back yard."

"Why do you want to do that?" His annoyance level was rising.

"Can we do it?"

"Follow me."

They took the stairs to the second floor. It was early evening with the sun setting behind them. With no lights to betray their presence, they stepped out onto a narrow balcony. Binoculars were on a table. In the dwindling light it was still easy to pick out the Barb Symonds's house. Security lights lined the back and around the pool. The dock had one at the entrance. No boat was anchored.

"Nice property," he said.

"She's had it for years. Maybe twenty. The house was here, but it needed a lot of work, which she did little by little. The lot next door was available, and she bought that as well."

"How long had you known her?"

"Since eighth grade."

"You weren't here when she had the accident?"

"I was on assignment in the Middle East at the time. There was chatter, but only for a few days, then it was gone. When they finally found her, her mother and her cousin Morgan took her to Palm Beach, had her cremated and that was it. I haven't been to the cemetery. I will go. Eventually."

Devon continued to stare at the back yard, hoping to see someone. Ray got up and headed inside. "There's someone who looks like Martin Edwards?"

Bradshaw came back to the balcony and took the binoculars. "It's him. So that's what he does when he comes to Marathon. Seeing that artist Chantal."

"How long has Martin been Sheriff'? I detected a type of maybe Boston accent in his speech."

"He's from Miami Dade as I understand it. He's not *the* sheriff. He's an adjunct sheriff. Special crimes type of thing."

Devon took the binoculars for one last look. She noticed a dog coming out the back door.

"It's Grace. Maybe. The German Shepherd. She's still there. She must be getting on six or seven by this time." She watched the dog for a minute more, then handed the binoculars back to Ray. "Thank you."

"I have to be in Sugarloaf Key tomorrow taking photos of a new development that's having a grand opening. I should be back by five, but I'll keep in touch." He tucked Devon's card with her cell phone number in his wallet.

✗   ✗   ✗   ✗   ✗

Ray Bradshaw gave her a bad feeling. There was an unpleasantness that ran deep and seeped out through his pores. The next day Ray's text came in around two o'clock. It said his contact from NOAA had a trailer on Big Pine Key and that's where he'd leave the photos. Then Ray texted again at three and said the developers wanted sunset photos so he couldn't be there until seven. He left directions.

After her last text from Ray, Devon opted for lunch. She was heading for the restaurant when she found her dad checking in.

"What a surprise!"

"You need backup after last night." He took his bag up to his room, then joined her in the restaurant.

"How's it coming along?" he asked.

"I met Martin Edwards. Two years ago he was the defense attorney for Barb in that government case. Of course he didn't mention it. Now he's a sheriff for Monroe County. I also met Ray Bradshaw. He was the first to go on board the *Sky Dragon* that Thursday. Has a house on the water. He took photos that Tuesday and got one of John Ryder's boat in the vicinity of Barb's. I sent it onto Mike at the Coast Guard."

"What's Edwards doing down here? It's got to be more than just a career change. He's connected to Ryder. So what are they into? By the way, did you see the birds when you were at the Symonds Gallery?"

"I did. Without a material analysis, I'd say they're Barbs. But... they can't be. The gallery had no Barb bird inventory two years back. The work is Chantal's. The problem is..." she tapped the table for emphasis "...if we accept that, then what about all the other birds? Are they Chantal's as well, and just labeled 'Barb Symonds'?"

"That would be a scandal no one would survive. Certainly worth killing over," her dad said.

"Oh, look at the time. We'll pick that up later. Gotta run. The sun's setting. I want to get out to the trailer before it does. What are you going to do?"

"I can't believe you trust this Ray guy. I'm going with you. There's a great little place called the No Name Bar. You can drop me off there. It's not far from where you're meeting Ray and you can pick me up on the way back. And I won't be far in case you need help."

"I won't need help."

✗ ✗ ✗ ✗ ✗

The back section of Big Pine Key was mainly pines and scrub grass. The sun was lower than the tops of the trees when Devon, following Ray's directions, pulled into the gravel driveway in front of a small dirty white trailer. Judging from the weeds, it had been in that spot a long time and without wheels would remain there.

Ray's car was parked along the road and lights were on inside the trailer. He was sitting at a table with a beer and a file folder in front of him. Judging from the kitchen, he brought the beer with him.

"Here's what I was able to get."

The setting gave Devon an uneasy feeling. Something was amiss, but she had no idea yet what it was. He slid the photos over as she sat down. They were satellite photos. Angled down it was possible to see the deck of John's boat as it was anchored next to the *Sky Dragon*. On the deck, near the railing, something was going on, but an enlargement or magnifying glass was needed.

"These are good. But a closeup would be better. I can enlarge it tomorrow. It's too late tonight." As she studied the photos, she suddenly noted that both had dates in small type in the corner. August 8th of two years ago. The Tuesday before Barb disappeared.

They were not printed today.

Immediately, Devon decided it was time to leave. Whatever game Ray Bradshaw was playing, it wasn't going to end well. Especially as she noted the gun with the silencer partially hidden by a magazine on the other chair beside him.

"You can see the two boats together, but nothing else. What do you think?"

How did he happen to have these from two years back? Was he helping or blackmailing someone? He still hadn't said anything.

"I need to head back. Meeting my dad for dinner." She stood. "I can enlarge them tomorrow. Give me a call. And thank you for doing this."

She hesitated, waiting for an answer. All she got was a nod.

The sheriff thought that Ray hired the two dudes from last night. Now she was positive. How far would she get? She pushed open the screen door and headed for her car. She made it to the driver-side door before the first shot rang out. It missed her head by inches and slammed into the back window. Without turning around or pulling out her gun, she got in, started the car, drove to the end of the street and turned left. She looked out the rear window and saw Bradshaw behind her.

There was still a band of orange above the horizon, but it wasn't giving off much light. Suddenly Devon knew she was going in the wrong direction. She needed to turn around. Going faster than she should have been, she was unprepared when the road suddenly sloped downhill.

It was nearly dark, but with what remained of the light, she could see that there was no normal end to the road. It just slid, without warning, into the Gulf of Mexico.

The change was so sudden she had no time to stop. Her brakes didn't work as the tires couldn't get traction and before she knew it, the car was sliding into the dark waters, soon to be totally submerged and carried away by a swift current.

"What the hell?" she screamed.

She tried opening the door, but the force of the water kept it closed. She grabbed her bag, and before the car totally went under, she was able to squeeze through the window she had thought to lower. The force of the car pulled her down but she pushed her way through the water to put distance between her and the descending vehicle.

When she surfaced, it was dark, but she could see a light through the trees that probably marked the end of the road. She swam toward it against the current. The closer she got to shore, the less powerful the current, making it easier for her to find footing.

As she got in sight of the light, she saw Ray Bradshaw standing on the road as it sloped down. Bastard, she thought. I'll get him for this.

To get close but not be seen, she had to climb ashore through the trees that grew down to the shoreline. Fearful of being heard, she silently inched her way, one branch at a time, until she could feel the land begin to rise. Keeping a line of shrubs between her and the road, she was able to get close to Bradshaw without him seeing her.

The street light, which had not been on before when she made her near fateful plunge, cast a glow over the area. She could see Bradshaw's every movement and right now he was on the cell phone.

"She did exactly what we thought," he said. She could hear his voice clearly. "Straight into the water. It was dark. Not a chance for her to get out. That should be the last of Devon January. Yeah. See you later."

While he spoke, Devon pulled her Smith and Wesson from her waterproof bag and aimed it at his head. At the last moment, he tilted forward as he finished his call.

In the moment she had to readjust her aim, another shot rang out and Bradshaw slid to the pavement. Devon froze. As she decided what to do, a man appeared.

He was pushing Bradshaw's car. He put Bradshaw into the driver's seat, closed the door and gave the car a shove. Under the streetlight, it slid slowly down the road until it disappeared into the darkened Gulf.

"He was a loose end," she said to herself putting her gun away. "Once I was gone, so was he."

Moments later, she heard a truck engine start, the exhausts making a racket in the still night air, then all went silent.

Hoping no one else was around, not caring about her wet clothes and hair, she made her way to the road and started back on foot the way she came. There were enough street lights that she wasn't in total darkness. She walked the distance to the trailer where she met Ray. The lights were still on. In theory she was dead, so no one would be looking for her. However, now being on the cautious side, she called her dad.

"I'm putting on the emergency signal so you'll know where I am. I don't have a car. It's a long story. Can you get a taxi or someone to drive you the short distance to pick me up. I'll be at the corner of Kyle and Deer." Not waiting for a yes or no, she ended the call.

She watched the trailer for a few moments, then took the chance and went inside. Still laying on the table were the two photos. Someone would be back to get them. She stuffed them inside the folder and stepped out in the moist night air. A few minutes later Don January arrived in an SUV.

"Our benefactor is heading to Key West, but graciously offered to take us back to Marathon."

"That's wonderful. How about Don Pedro's," Devon said of the Mexican restaurant.

Her dad stared as he looked at her. She patted her hair and wiped a piece of grass, she hoped it was grass, from her face.

"A date that didn't go well," she said. She laughed.

The driver, refusing cash or a drink, left them off at the restaurant, then headed back over the seven-mile bridge.

"What on earth happened to you?" He looked at her in astonishment. "Do you really want to go for dinner?"

"Swimming in the Gulf of Mexico really kicks up one's appetite."

✗   ✗   ✗   ✗   ✗

After dinner, after a shower and clean clothes and finishing a glass of wine, Devon said, "I'd like to see this through tonight. They won't be expecting me. I'm referring to the wonderful folks like Justin Walker, Martin Edwards, Morgan Price and Chantal."

"Will we need backup?"

"Definitely. Call my friend the Chief." She handed him the card.

✗   ✗   ✗   ✗   ✗

Bradshaw's boat was where she saw it last. It was a short ride across the inlet. The only lights as they approached Barb's back yard from the dock were the pool lights. The rest of the back property had only the glow of a single pole light. Her dad had done his reconnaissance of the front. Two cars out front. And one in the garage.

"So you think you have the answer. The one that's eluded all law enforcement for the past two years?"

"Yes. They should have paid attention to Grace."

"I guess I didn't know Grace as well as you did."

"Mike and I had the answer this morning. The murder went down on Tuesday, not Wednesday. And not from the *Sky Dragon*, but from John Ryder's boat. Those photos Ray showed that something was being moved from Ryder's boat into the water. The *Sky Dragon* was a red herring. Where's the Chief?"

"He'll be right by the gate. Ready?"

They walked around to the front where Devon knocked.

"I don't hear the dog," he said.

"She knows it's me." Devon smiled.

The door opened. Devon couldn't decide who had the more astonished look: her dad, or the woman who greeted them.

"When did you know?" He turned to his daughter.

Devon looked at the tall attractive dark-haired woman and smiled.

"Hi Barb," she said. "Can we come in?"

The woman stood there staring. "You're dead."

"That's one hell of a greeting," Don said.

He stepped around her as every emotion Barb Symonds could muster flashed across her face. She finally moved away from the door. Behind her with guns pulled was Martin Edwards and Morgan Price.

"No one knew," Barb said. Her fury was nearly out of control. "The perfect crime. How did you?"

"Grace knew. I was at Ray's spying on you. I saw Grace come out and hug your leg. She truly didn't like Chantal. The thing with the two boats was clever. Had us going for a while. So how'd it go with Chantal? John just invited her to go on a cruise down here. Gave her a wine with a sedative and once she was out, over the side she went. That's what it looks like in the satellite photos Ray Bradshaw had. Was he blackmailing someone?"

"Our artifact forgery business was going so well. Chantal got greedy. Got stupid. Made mistakes and that brought the government down on me. Me! That was unforgivable. Thank goodness Martin came to the rescue, otherwise that prosecuting attorney would have put me in jail forever. I had no choice but to disappear."

Devon stood looking at her for something that was no longer there. "We were such good friends. What happened?"

"Were we? It was a long time ago. I'm sorry."

For a moment, Devon actually believed her.

Don, who had been holding his cell phone said, "Now would be a good time."

"You brought reinforcements," Barb said, looking surprised.

"It was the least I could do. Especially after the incident at Big Pine Key. My death... just another accident. I can't believe you tried to kill me. What happened? I thought we were such good friends."

✗

Dianne Neral Ell has written professionally for trade and consumer publications, online magazines and websites. Her short stories have appeared in anthologies and *Sherlock Holmes Mystery Magazines*. *The Exhibit*, a novel of crime and suspense, is currently available at most retailers including Amazon and Barnes and Noble. She is a member of the Mystery Writers of America, the Author's Guild and the Florida Writers Association. Her website is: www.dianneneralell.com.

THE STRANGE DISAPPEARANCE OF THE TALKING HORSE

by Ron Goulart

The assassination attempt was rather novel and a bit lackluster.

It was a moderately misty London evening in late April of 1903. Harry Challenge left his suite at the Grand Babylon Hotel on the Strand some minutes before 7 p.m. and was walking at a somewhat leisurely pace along St. Martin's Lane toward his client's hotel.

He was a lean, moderately tanned man in his middle thirties and in the breast pocket of his conservative dark suit was the cablegram that sent him on his new assignment.

It said: *Dear son: That enormously rich showman Colonel Milford Bascom is again hunting attractions for his Manhattan Museum of Marvels, that mecca of gullible halfwits. We took the old boy for a splendid fee when you located that missing automaton a few years back. This time he's looking for, so help me, a talking horse. Let us fleece him yet again. Meet him at the Imperial-British Hotel at 7 p.m. on Tuesday night. Your loving father, The Challenge International Detective Agency.*

The night mist was growing a bit thicker and a bit colder. On the Thames a few mournful foghorns bellowed. Harry patted his pocket. "I hope the Colonel hasn't brought that damn midget with him this time." There were few other walkers, just one hansom cab came rattling, its horse clopping.

He was passing a row of small shops, each of them closed. All at once the wide dusty window of Chadwick's Curiosity Shop blossomed with bright electric light, illuminating, among other things, a dangling trio of puppets, a stuffed possum, two yellowed death masks, a scroll loosely tied with faded red ribbon, two clear wine bottles with messages in them and a large, green, goggle-eyed toad who might have been alive.

The wide, plain wood door snapped open outward. There was a very pretty blond young woman standing there. She was wearing a thin lacy night dress that had two growing red splotches below her partially visible breasts. Her dark hair was disheveled, her face a grayish pale. "I wonder, sir, if you—" Then, her eyes snapping shut, she started to fall toward him.

He didn't catch her, instead he leaped backward and yanked his .38 revolver out of his shoulder holster. "You shouldn't try to hide a pistol beneath a night dress that flimsy, ma'am," he advised. "It'll almost always show."

Muttering, the woman called, "Eric, Nigel."

Out of the wide doorway came a large, wide man wearing a black hood with ragged eyeholes. He was clutching an axe, raising it to take a swing at the detective. "We're going to do you dirt, Harry."

Harry shot this first lout in the left thigh.

"Blimey," exclaimed Eric as he started to fall. He smacked into the bloody woman, who had just about succeeded in getting herself upright.

"Damn it, Eric."

The second large assassin made his way outside, barely dodging his two associates. "The game ain't worth the candle, Guv," he said as he started running off into the encroaching fog.

"Are you about finished putting on your exhibition of the manly arts, nitwit?"

About a quarter of a block away a small man in evening clothes was standing beside a parked hansom.

After pausing to pick up his fallen bowler hat and dust off the brim with his sleeve, Harry called, "Major Nemo, what a pleasant surprise. I'll join you in a moment."

To the jostled girl he said, "Who hired you?"

Very softly she replied, "A toff, sir. He gave us ten pounds, showed us pictures of you and told us about when you'd be passing this way."

"A name, a description."

"Never gave us a name. Was an average-sized gentleman around sixty years of age and nowhere near as good-looking as you."

Grinning a thin grin, he told her, "If you or your brood ever try to ambush me again, I'm really going to get mad. Now begone with you." He left her and walked down to the Major and the cab. "Did I mention what a pleasant surprise this is?"

The top-hatted midget said in his piping voice, "Oh, sure, you're just overjoyed to see me. That's why you're squinting at me like I'm the guy who triggered the Bubonic Plague." Major Nemo was a bit over three feet tall and clad in a spotless suit of evening clothes.

"Well, not quite that degree of fondness," admitted Harry. "Did your boss send you to meet me?"

"Righto, I got the latrine duty tonight." Doffing his topper, he indicated the hansom cab. "I had to promise the driver we'd pay to have the gig fumigated before he agreed to let you set foot in his cab."

"Why the transportation?"

"The fatboy's got a yen to dine at a new joint, so he wants to have his chinwag with you there and not at our posh and zealously-overpriced hotel."

"Any idea who might've hired those second-rate assassins?"

The Major puckered his face. "We are not, dumbbell, the only chaps looking for Dobbins. Some of the competitors are what street urchins in Manhattan would call dickheads."

"Who the hell is Dobbins? And what competition?"

"The sahib is prepared to explain all to you at least three times," said Major Nemo. "So what say we hoist our backsides into the royal coach, Cinderella, and make haste to join the inflated impresario at Maxine's Superior Cuisine Hideaway."

"Catchy name," observed Harry as he followed the feisty Major into the waiting cab.

✗ ✗ ✗ ✗ ✗

Maxine's was trying mightily to look like a cozy French inn. There was a deep sooty fireplace with a kettle perking on the hob, a moderately obese tabby dozing on the mantel and three handsome waiters in peasant attire that looked not more than a day back from the laundry.

Colonel Bascom was an abundantly portly man with a large quantity of fluffy white hair and whiskers. He had a borderline russet complexion and a suit of large red and gold checks. He wiped his plump face with a napkin, cleared his throat and spoke. "That was a most satisfying meal, gentlemen, on all counts, from the appetizer to the inventive dessert. A choice selection of viands fit for—"

"The old gink means he liked it." Six assorted bound volumes of *Punch* from 1893 to 1897 had been stacked on the Major's rustic chair to lift him up to a dining position.

Harry tapped his forefinger on his brandy glass. "The meal's over, so tell me about the missing talking horse."

"I fear," said the showman, adding more sugar to his coffee, "that I may have been too terse in my cable to your esteemed father in far-off Manhattan, the bustling metropolis oft known as Baghdad on the Hudson, and given the impression that we are seeking a living, breathing, talking horse. Nay, not so, on the contrary. This exceptional stallion is a remarkable example of an automaton, a mechanical animal of astounding—"

"He means it's a doozy," added the Major, shifting uncomfortably on the topmost bound volume. "When he gets that gadget on display at the Museum of Miracles in New York, the rubes will come flocking. Myself, I prefer the hootchie cootchie babes at Coney Island."

Harry, smiling thinly at the Major, suggested, "Hush."

The Colonel reached across to pat Major Nemo atop his middle-parted hair. "Yes, my dear Major, shut your yap for a spell," he advised. "Now then, our mechanical horse is named Dobbins."

"Then you were not in on the creation of this Dobbins?"

"The Colonel is no mechanical genius. He can't even—"

"Ahem, my dear Major. This incredible mechanical talking horse was the invention of the late Dr. Horace Bellerman, formerly of the Advanced Science Department of the Barset Academy in Barsetshire." He ran a plump hand through his feathery hair. "He constructed this magnificent creature in the late autumn of 1897 and displayed it to his colleagues and some newsmen. Then, for reasons I have been completely unable to discern, both he and Dobbins dropped from sight. There were rumors that he had a silent partner named Theo Culhane, who was no better than he should be and ended up in Fennimore Prison in Sussex."

"Theo Culhane is no longer behind bars," said Harry.

The Colonel scowled. "Ah, I had not heard that."

"He escaped two weeks ago and the newspapers gave it quite a play here in England, since up to then Fennimore had been considered impossible to escape from."

Major Nemo again shifted on his book-top position and made a couple of small bounces. "Your gab is all just fascinating, but get back to the blooming tin horse."

"For once you are pertinent, Major. Yes, a few weeks ago I received a cable from a young woman named Maud Bellerman, a niece of the good doctor and his only heir," continued the Colonel. "She knew I was interested in acquiring this astounding and *nonpareil* automated creature and she offered to sell it to my fabled Manhattan Museum of Marvels for a tidy sum."

"He's rolling in tidy sums," added Nemo. "But my salary is what double-dome economists would call *un*tidy."

"Major, as the epitome of littleness, the ultimate in compactness, my admiration of you knows no bounds, but again I must request that you please shut your bazoo." The Colonel returned his attention to Harry. "But by the time we reached Albion's green and pleasant shores, Maud Bellerman vanished from human ken and we turned once again to the Challenge International Detective Agency."

"Yet another example that his poor old brain is seriously befuddled," suggested the Major, bouncing noisily on his pile of *Punch*.

Harry inquired, "Where was Maud supposed to be?"

"She is a teacher of American Literature at the London Academy for Cultured Young Women and—"

"They don't know where their wandering schoolmarm is," the Major contributed.

With extreme patience the showman said, "I must again suggest, my dear little Major, that you take a vow of silence. I'm sure that friend Harry has further questions."

"Yep, I do," he replied. "First off, tell me who might be hiring masked men to keep me from finding this damned horse."

Bascom, frowning, sipped his coffee. "While I do have rivals who'd like to display this astonishing mechanical steed in vaudeville houses and traveling carnivals throughout the length and breadth of the United States, I think that—"

"But killing me to keep me from locating the gadget seems a bit excessive," Harry put in.

The Major bounced once and raised a forefinger. "Suppose," he suggested, "this nag is valuable for some other reason."

"Yeah, maybe something having to do with this Theo Culhane guy." Harry pushed back in his chair. "I think I'll have a talk with Inspector Beggarstaff of Scotland Yard." He stood, put on his hat and left the place.

✗　✗　✗　✗　✗

Inspector Beggarstaff was dapper and handsome, as he well knew, and he came striding confidently out of the misty night and into the smoky sedate Gentleman's Londontown Pub. While doffing his deerstalker cap and shifting his grip on the weathered briefcase under his arm, he spotted Harry at a darkwood booth on the right-hand side of the half-empty drinking establishment.

"Jolly good to see you again, old man," he said as he deposited his cap and overcoat on a brass coat rack. "And allow me to say that I'll be damned happy to help you out with this new mystery you're having such a pesky time with."

"Appreciate that." Harry shook hands with the tall, lean Inspector.

Seating himself opposite the detective and placing his briefcase precisely atop the table, he said, "Allow me to state at the outset, old boy, that I bear you and that personable reporter Miss Jennie Barr no ill will about the way you two managed to garner the lion's share of the credit for capturing Dr. Grimshaw a few months ago."

Harry grinned. "I had nothing much to do with all the London newspapers paying most of their attention to Jennie and me. She's a first-rate American journalist and when she's in London, well, her colleagues on the English press are eager to—"

"All water under the bridge, my dear chap. Although seeing headlines like *Barr & Challenge Capture Notorious Dr. Grimshaw* did cause me some pain at the time, since my men and I did play an important part in the apprehending of that criminal mastermind. But… oh, well, let us forget it."

Nodding in agreement, Harry said, "Okay, so what can you tell me about the disappearance of Maud Bellerman?"

Beggarstaff lit his briar pipe. "I'm very much afraid that this affair is much more complicated and dangerous, old man, than you perhaps realize."

"Oh, so?"

Opening his briefcase, the Inspector extracted a pale blue folder. He held up a brown-tinted photograph. "This is what your police in the States call a mug shot, I believe."

"And who's the ample lady?"

"Her name is Ophelia Dragonwyck and at the moment we at the Yard categorize her as one of the three most dangerous women in the world."

The woman in full view and profile shot was fat, impressively so. She had a black widow spider tattooed on her wide, flabby forehead.

"She weighs," continued the Inspector, "a shade over 300 pounds. She's been involved in wide-ranging criminal activities in Tangiers. Murder for hire is a specialty of hers. She usually kills her victims by dropping on them from above and squelching them to death."

"Tangiers. She must also be dealing in drugs."

Nodding forlornly, Beggarstaff continued. "Yes, chiefly hashish. And also prostitution, smuggling, blackmail, grand theft, and forgery."

"How does she fit into the mess I'm working on?"

"She and Theo Culhane were lovers at one time. She is also said to practice black magic and may have used that to extract the bloke from his prison cell."

"Love knows no boundaries," observed Harry. "Does she work with a gang?"

"About five blackguards. The chief of which is a nasty bit of goods named Salazar Alhambra. We haven't a photograph of him, but he's said to have a terribly small nose."

"How does Ophelia fit into all this mess?"

"She is apparently back in London along with Culhane and looking for something of considerable value." The Inspector paused to relight his pipe. "It has long been my suspicion that the late Dr. Bellerman may also have been involved with Theo Culhane in some smuggling and burglary activities."

Harry frowned. "You have proof of this?"

"Let me just say, old chap, that I have a strong hunch." He paused. "You haven't heard anything about black pearls?"

"Nope, and I wasn't hired to find such stuff. I'm just looking for a talking horse. I'd like to see the place where Maud Bellerman was living."

From a coat pocket Beggarstaff produced a silver key. "Nothing there, old boy, but feel free to nose around."

"Now that we've arrived at a *détente*, we'll share information. Right?"

"But of course, Harry. I'll share with you, you'll share with me."

"Absolutely," replied Harry, sounding almost sincere.

✗   ✗   ✗   ✗   ✗

The late night still had its thick fog and added a fair amount of rain. As Harry approached the ornate glass doors of the Grand Babylon Hotel and started to cross the damp sidewalk, he heard someone mention his name, more or less.

"I got to see 'Arry Challenge, I tell you." A thin boy of about thirteen was facing the massive uniformed doorman. "I got a bloomin' message for 'im." He was clad in a much-patched reefer jacket and his trousers had long since faded to a pale shade of blue.

The doorman's uniform consisted of a knee-length coat of royal blue with an abundance of large gold buttons and an impressive set of gold-tasseled épaulets. The golden fringe began to flicker as the big man, taking hold of the boy's coat, started to shake him. "You best be gone, boy, before I give you the vigorous thrashing your rude behavior deserves."

Harry tapped the man on his upper arm. "I suggest," he said evenly, "that you don't attempt anything like that. Otherwise I'll probably thrash *you*. Or cold-cock you as well."

"Sir, this ragamuffin is—"

"I'm Harry Challenge," he said to the boy as the doorman let him go. "You have a message for me?"

"Blimey, I do, Guv." From inside his coat he withdrew a pristine square pinkish envelope.

"Who from?"

"A bloke give me a penny to deliver it. But I'd guess it's a billydoo from a lady since it smells like a bunch o' flowers."

Accepting the missive, Harry gave the boy a shilling. "Know who the bloke was?"

"Never seen 'im before until this very night. But not a toff like yourself." He deposited the coin in one serviceable coat pocket, touched a forefinger to his lock and retreated into the night fog.

"My apologies, sir," said the doorman. "I had no idea you were expecting a message from a street urchin."

Harry studied the man for a few seconds. "Aren't you Sir Robert Delmar, the financier?"

Nodding sadly, the doorman replied, "Alas, I am. But I have somewhat fallen from grace, I'm afraid."

Harry started toward the hotel doors.

"Don't make the same mistake that I did. I ruined my life, Mr. Challenge," warned the big man. "Never enter into a clandestine affair with a lady acrobat."

"That's one of my cardinal rules of life, Sir Robert," he said.

When he was seated in one of the vast lobby's many fat armchairs, Harry opened the envelope. It contained a large yellow ticket for tomorrow's 2:30 matinee at the Picadilly Music Hall and a scented note.

The note, in a polite feminine hand, said: *You'll enjoy my turn on tomorrow's afternoon matinee. I am third on the bill and afterwards we must have a chat in my dressing room. We can have a very pleasant equine conversation. Cordially, Tilda Merrydew.*

✗　✗　✗　✗　✗

The plump middle-aged woman who managed the building where the missing Bellerman girl lived was, for some reason, dressed in a bright-colored Gypsy outfit, complete with crimson headscarf and dangling golden earrings. She was on her hands and knees on the gray hall carpet as Harry, using the key he'd borrowed from Beggarstaff the night before, let himself into the building. There was a substantial scattering of Tarot cards on the carpeting. The door of her flat stood half open.

Looking up at him in the way of someone who ought to wear glasses but doesn't, she asked, "And who might you be? But I must say you're much too dapper and upstanding-looking to be a cat burglar."

"If you think I'm dapper, you ought to see Inspector Beggarstaff, who gave me this key," he said. "And were I a cat burglar, I'd have come in over the rooftops, ma'am."

"You're from Scotland Yard, then?" She picked up the *Knight of Wands* card, dropped it into her large flowered reticule. "I spilled the whole blooming deck of them. I'm frightfully clumsy most mornings."

"Actually, I'm a private inquiry agent." Kneeling, he scooped up some cards, including the *Queen of Pentacles* and the *Ace of Wands*. "I'd like permission to take a look at Miss Bellerman's rooms."

"Yes, of course. I'd show you myself, except that I'm already late for my work at the Otherworldly Tea Shop on Wilder's Walk, just off the Strand. I'm the resident fortune teller and there I'm called Madam Xenobia." Acquiring the last of the cards and stowing them in the reticule, she got to her feet with a little help from the detective. "Do you have any notion as to the poor girl's whereabouts?"

"Not as yet. What do you think about her disappearance?"

She shook her head, the large earrings fluttering. "Not an awful lot, I fear. But Maud has been awfully nervous these past few weeks."

"Know why?"

"Alas, no, she never confided anything in me," she replied. "But I did notice on at least two or three occasions a strange man dressed all in black standing across the street near the postal box and almost certainly watching this house."

"Strange how?"

"Well, he was obviously a foreigner, some sort of dago. And he had the smallest nose I've ever seen." She tapped her own nose with a forefinger. "A terribly small nose."

"Did Maud talk about any man with a terribly small nose? Did she see him?"

"If the poor lass did, she never told me about him," the fortune teller said. "I must be up and doing. Should you ever be in the vicinity of the Otherworldly Tea Shop, drop in and I'll tell your fortune without my usual fee. The tea, however, you'll have to pay for, I'm afraid."

"You missed the *Ace of Cups*." Harry returned the Tarot card to Madam Xenobia.

✗ ✗ ✗ ✗ ✗

The fortune-telling manager hadn't mentioned that Maud's room was in a state of considerable disorder. Every drawer, bureau, desk, and what-have-you, had been pulled out and dumped on the floor. Letters, typed pages, sketches, bills, and memos were thick on the imitation Persian rug. A Tiffany lamp, partially injured, lay on its side next to a fallen bell glass that held a small Venus, this one with arms, and was leaning against a brass waste basket. Next to that was a pamphlet from *Balderstone's Stables—Rotten Row's Best Horse Rental Establishment. For Gentlemen and Lady Equestrians*. Written about that in brown ink was the inscription *Your friend and admirer John B*. Harry folded the pamphlet and slipped it into a coat pocket.

The rest of the rooms had been searched, more than likely by Ophelia Dragonwyck's minions to find some clue as to the present whereabouts of the elusive Dobbins; they had been quite thorough.

In the bright white kitchen, a pale blue teapot sat on a deal table. In a single matching teacup were the dregs of tea lying in the bottom. "Wonder what Madam Xenobia would make of these tea leaves?" Harry checked his pocket watch, made a quick final survey of the flat and left.

✗   ✗   ✗   ✗   ✗

Harry's complimentary ducat entitled him to a box seat on the right-hand side of the Picadilly Music Hall, a huge theatre of slightly faded opulence. High in the domed ceiling was suspended a trio of large glittering hanging chandeliers. The one nearest his box was missing several tear-shaped bulbs and two of the surviving ones were flickering and emitting an occasional faint sizzling sound.

Since he was the only occupant, Harry placed his homburg on the empty purple plush seat next to him.

The act preceding Tilda Merrydew was, according to the large placard on the easel set up on the edge of the bare stage: *Lazlo & His Magic Guitar. "Just Back From a Triumphant Tour of the Capitals of Middle Europe!"*

Lazlo was a moderately overweight young man wearing a loose-fitting suit of evening clothes and a curly blond wig that didn't quite fit.

The magical part applied to the fact that he was also a pretty fair juggler. At the moment he was juggling his silver-fronted twelve-string guitar, some heavily-annotated sheets of music, two Indian clubs, and a tasseled red fez. He caught the fez, tassel flickering, as it went by, plopped it on his head, grabbed the music and tossed it on a nearby folding table, plucked the Indian clubs out of the air and sent them spinning backstage. Finally, he caught the guitar, swiftly tuned it and then played one of the Goldberg Variations in Flamenco style.

There was quite a bit of approving whistling and yells of satisfaction drifting out of the smoky first balcony. When some of the music hall began shouting, "Encore! Encore!" Harry consulted his pocket watch.

But Lazlo demurred, sent a few kisses out across the footlights and took himself and his magic guitar off the stage.

The next placard was changed by a young man in an usher uniform. It proclaimed: *Tilda Merrydew, The Bawdy Nightingale of Picadilly.*

She was even better received than the guitarist/juggler and was given an enthusiastic standing ovation before she even set foot on the boards.

A spotlight sent a huge yellow circle onto the darkened stage and Tilda came hopping into it. She was a very pretty young woman in her middle twenties, red-haired and, unlike some lady singers of bawdy songs, slender. She wore a simple floor-length gray skirt, a pale yellow buff-sleeved blouse, and a small flowered yellow straw hat. "Hey now, shut up, will you?" she shouted. "I sure as blazes can't wait all the bloomin' night to start me catterwalling, can I? Now c' mon, give a poor working gel a chance."

Gradually quiet prevailed and after a few final cries of "We love you, Tildy!" she began to sing. Her voice was strong and indicated to the detective that Tilda had considerable musical training.

She sang "Me Sailor Left Me Standin' at the Bloomin' Church Door and Sailed Away," "Ever' Time 'e Kisses Me, It Gets Me Dander Up!" and, donning a top-hat, "I'm Burlington Bertie and I Sleeps Till Ten-Thirty."

Midway through her act, Harry, who by now had seen photos of the vanished Bellerman woman, told himself, "Damn, without the lower-class touches and that godawful orange wig, Tilda well could be the missing Maud."

The dressing-room door had a large golden star painted on it and below that was a half-sheet of vellum on which was lettered *Miss Tilda Merrydew* in Baskerville Bold type.

Opening his coat so he could get at his revolver faster, Harry knocked politely.

The door opened about six inches and the redheaded singer, after looking him over, invited, "Do come in, Mr. Challenge."

"Since you've dropped the Cockney accent, why not shed the wig, Miss Bellerman?"

Smiling, she opened the door wider and stepped back. "I imagined you'd recognize me."

"Some of the folks who are intent on finding you may also tumble to your disguise." He crossed the threshold, shutting the door.

The dressing room had a faint floral scent and a large illuminated makeup mirror with a large opaque folding screen of floral pattern silk planted next to it. "I established this alter ego over a year ago," she told him as she stepped behind the screen to change out of the Tilda Merrydew outfit.

"Why, exactly?" He straddled the straight-back chair before the mirror.

"It had nothing to do with hiding out, originally," she said as she tossed her blouse onto the top of the screen. "I've always been a pretty good singer and decided to try for a sideline career that was a bit more exciting than to explain Mark Twain, Nathaniel Hawthorne, and Henry James to a pack of over-privileged school girls. I've been appearing in music halls for nearly a year and fitting it in with my teaching schedule."

"When you stopped being a teacher and left your flat, that made you difficult for Colonel Bascom to find and acquire Dobbins."

"I had to become Tilda full-time when I realized I was in danger." The young woman stepped out from behind the screen wearing a quiet plaid traveling suit. Her hair was now blond. "Some very nasty people seem to be eager to get hold of Dobbins."

"Where is he?" Harry was standing facing the young woman.

She smiled. "Oh, I got a notion from another of your American writers. From Edgar Allan Poe's 'The Purloined Letter.' And I hid him in plain sight."

"We can collect him later. Tell me about these nasty people."

"Would you care for a cup of tea?"

"Not especially."

"Feel free to smoke."

"I quit several months ago. And I don't want a biscuit."

Maud sighed. "I really don't know their names," she explained, sitting in the chair he'd vacated. "A week-and-a-half ago, while I was having lunch alone at a tea shop near the school, a very fat woman sat down across from me uninvited and said, 'It will go much easier with you, dear child, if you sell the horse to us and not that American buffoon.'"

"Did this obese lady have a black widow spider tattooed on her forehead?"

She inhaled sharply. "You know her?"

"I've never met her, but Scotland Yard sure knows her," he answered. "Her name is Ophelia Dragonwyck and she's considered one of the most dangerous female master criminals in Europe."

Maud folded her arms, then unfolded them. "Why would an international crook be interested in my horse?" She folded her arms again.

"I don't think it's because she wants someone to talk to. Look, is there something maybe hidden inside Dobbins?"

"No, that's not possible. I mean, Uncle Horace taught me how to take care of him and see that all his gears and his steam engine and his vocal equipment are in good shape." She rose up, sat down. "The point is, Harry, there's no room in his metal carcass to stash much of anything."

"So what else did Ophelia have to say?"

"Well, when I told her that I had already made an arrangement with Colonel Bascom, she took hold of my wrist." The young woman rubbed her left wrist. "Squeezed very tightly. 'You'll never sell it to that mountebank, my dear. Not if you wish to remain among the living.' She said they would pay a hundred pounds and that there must be no haggling on my part."

Harry moved beside Maud, placed a hand on her shoulder. "When was this exchange to take place?"

"She gave me forty-eight hours and then someone would call on me and if I tried to elude them or ask the police for help, I might as well just walk over to London Bridge right then and jump into the Thames, because that would be a much more comfortable way to die."

"But you headed here, instead. And Dobbins is still safely hidden?"

"There's an old tunnel in the basement of my building. I got out that way."

"All right, now we have to—"

"There's one other thing and that scared me quite a lot." She reached out, taking hold of his hand. "There was a man who came into the tea shop and stood just inside the doorway, waiting for the fat lady." She inhaled again, shook her head. "He was a large, wide Spaniard and had a terribly small nose."

"That would be a chap named Salazar Alhambra."

"Another criminal mastermind?"

"Nope, one of Ophelia's thugs," Harry said. "This might be an apt time to go gather up Dobbins."

"It would," she agreed. "I'll go explain to the manager that I can't do the evening show."

"Will he get angry?"

"No, 'e'll just try to grab me fanny."

"I'll take a look around backstage and make sure we aren't suffering from any lurkers."

While the young woman headed for the manager's office, Harry explored the shadowy area behind the stage. Out in front of the footlights two lady acrobats in spangled tights were swinging from trapezes while the small brass band tootled. "Could one of those lasses be the woman who ruined Sir Robert's life?"

Harry heard a rustling sound over in a darkened area where a large steamer trunk was stored. He'd taken a few steps into the darkness when he became aware of a booted foot scraping on the boards behind him.

As he turned, going for his .38 revolver, a wide man with a very small nose swung a heavy Indian club against Harry's right temple. He couldn't quite get hold of the gun and the second hard blow to his head caused him to stumble, lose the power to walk, and then fall. The sound of the brass band all at once died and the darkness became complete.

Awakening, coughing, and with the harsh odor of smelling salts in his nostrils and a throbbing pain at the back of his skull, Harry became aware that he was being fanned by a small top-hat.

"C'mon, c'mon, Hawkshaw, up and at 'em," urged a piping voice. "Quit playing possum and find us our horse."

"As I live and breathe, darned if it isn't my chum, the one and only Major Nemo. How come our paths are crossing once again?"

"I, too, am a detective, though not a clunk like you, Challenge." The diminutive man returned his topper to his head. "I've been following your peregrinations through this crackpot city since early in the day, unnoticed by you, lummox. Wanted to see if you were earning that piece of highway robbery you and your dear old pappy call a fee."

Also in the backstage area where Harry had been conked were Lazlo, the guitar-playing juggler, and a concerned pink-faced man in his late fifties. "I'm Dr. Steinberg, Mr. Challenge, and unless this offensive little chap is a friend of the family, I suggest we have him shooed out of the theatre."

"It's *you*, Sawbones, who can take a hike," suggested Nemo, making an unpleasant sound with his tongue against his upper lip. "I intend to stick with this guy until we find this dippy broad and her vastly overrated tin nag."

Harry, with the aid of the juggler, sat up. "I dismissed my hansom when I got to the music hall. I'm going to have to get a jitney cab now, so—"

"No need, Challenge," said the Major. "I'll fetch us one and then we can work on the case in tandem."

"It occurs to me, Major," Harry said as he got to his feet on his own, "that I may have a use for you. So do get us a cab."

"Your wish is my command, bozo." Nemo went hurrying toward the egress to the street.

"I advise you not to travel with that obnoxious person," said the doctor.

"I also advise you not to," Lazlo seconded.

"Yeah, don't do it," said one of the spangled acrobats.

As Harry and the Major were driven away from the music hall, the grayness of the afternoon sky deepened, the mist grew thicker and rain came hitting down hard on the roof of their jitney.

Nemo removed his top-hat, rested it on his lap and remarked, "Okay, Old Sleuth, what screwball scheme have you got cooking in your coco?"

Harry said, "We're heading for Rotten Row and—"

"Hey, I deduced that when I heard you tell that to the cabman. Do you have a sudden yen to go horseback riding with the swells?"

"Nope. Actually, I have a hunch that Dobbins is there at Balderstone's Stables."

"Geez, I feel just like Dr. Watson asking Holmes questions. Why in the bloody blue blazes do you think that?"

Harry explained the signed Balderstone pamphlet he'd found at Maud's flat and her remarks about Edgar Allan Poe and hiding things in plain sight.

"Poe, is that the gink who married his sister and was a hophead?"

Harry said, "It occurred to me that a stable would be a good place to hide a horse among a bunch of other horses."

"Dobbins does look pretty much like a real horse," the Major admitted. "If this guy Balderstone is a pal of Miss Maudie, maybe he would stash that tin nag there for her."

"You can poke around the stables while I'm talking to Balderstone and see whether you can spot Dobbins. Balderstone may be reluctant to admit he's got the horse."

"Sneaky poking around is a specialty of mine," the Major admitted. "So say we find our wandering horse, what then?"

"We'll get him out of there."

"Because you're afraid whoever has Maud will force her to tell them where Dobbins is?"

"Yeah." Harry figured that if he had the talking horse he could use him as a bargaining chip to get the girl back, but he didn't want to mention that to the Major.

He told their driver the address for the Balderstone stables.

⤢　⤢　⤢　⤢　⤢

Balderstone's Riding Stables consisted of a large white-painted barnlike building that looked to hold about a dozen-and-a-half stalls and was fronted by a wide strip of turf.

As Harry's cab drove up and stopped, a large closed wagon with *Fellows & Creech Horse Transporting* lettered in red on its side came shooting out of the barn, drawn by two Percherons and with a man with a very small nose in the driver's seat.

It nearly slammed into their cab and went rattling onto the road. Hopping out, Harry called to the driver, "I'd like to borrow your cab. How much?"

"Well, now, sir, I don't right—"

"Twenty pounds."

"You've got yourself a deal, sir. And you'll bring me horse and it back here?"

"Guaranteed."

Taking the money, the driver climbed down.

As Harry boosted himself up into the seat and took hold of the reins, Major Nemo came scrambling up to join him. "Half a moment, Challenge. I'm going to ride shotgun." He was holding his Derringer.

"Okay, but little or no conversation." He got the cab turned around and gave chase.

✗   ✗   ✗   ✗   ✗

The parlor in which Maud awakened a few hours earlier was tall and thin. At first she thought she had gone color blind. The sofa she was laid out on was black, the carpet was white, the wallpaper consisted of wide black-and-white stripes. Six large black-and-white posters in art nouveau style by Aubrey Beardsley were hung with white frames on the nearest wall in an even row at eye level.

But then she noticed on a small round white table across the room a short stack of back issues of *The Yellow Book*. The covers were a bright yellow and, very briefly, that cheered her up.

The black doorknob in the white door gave a faint rattling click. The door swung open outward and an average-sized man with a fringe of curly black hair above his ears and a nondescript face crossed the threshold. His suit was white, his bowtie black. He smiled in a way that did not validate his attempt to be affable. "Maud, dear, I can't understand why we haven't gotten together for so many years."

"I think, Theo, that's because you've been serving so much time in some of the world's best-known prisons."

"I suppose that is one of the reasons, my dear," Theo Culhane admitted. "But since I am such a well-known criminal mastermind, I am obliged to plan and commit a certain number of mastermind crimes to justify my title. Now and again Scotland Yard, unfortunately, manages to run me down. And on one rather embarrassing occasion, even the Royal Canadian Mounted Police did."

"How did you know I was Tilda Merrydew?"

"We have all sorts of minions who beat the bushes for us, dear Maudie. Only a matter of time, you see, until we find anyone we want."

"And now you want my uncle's talking horse. Are you planning to go into competition with Colonel Bascom?"

The escaped mastermind chuckled deep in his throat. "I don't happen to be, like that demented showman, a collector of useless freaks and gadgets." He paused and rubbed his white-gloved hands together three times. "What I am interested in, what the light of my life, Ophelia, is interested in most deeply are the Marinoff Black Pearls. That is—"

"What in the devil are the Marinoff Black Pearls? I've never heard of them."

"Oh, really? That's odd, because Dobbins is the only one who knows where they are." Bowing, her father's erstwhile partner left the parlor and relocked the white door.

✗   ✗   ✗   ✗   ✗

About a half-hour later, a very loud thumping began at a distance from the parlor wherein Maud was a prisoner. The noise grew louder, produced by two booted feet coming closer.

The walls of the black-and-white room shook, the white door rattled. Then it was booted open.

An immense woman of some forty-five years stood on the threshold, jiggling slightly. Her short-cropped hair was a pale orange, her flushed face was perspiring, and the black widow spider tattooed on her forehead was tilting to the left.

"Ah, we meet again." Ophelia Dragonwyck's white dress was long and flowing, a pair of quite large black boots showed below the lacy hem. "I was certainly not planning, you whey-faced little poppet, to waste the remains of my day using hot pokers and similar doohickeys on you," she announced after clearing her throat with two loud barking coughs. "However, my estimable paramour Theo has informed me that you have no intention of telling us a blessed thing about the thirteen perfectly matched Marinoff Black Pearls."

"But I don't *know* a blessed thing about pearls, black or otherwise, Miss Dragonwyck."

"*Mrs*. Dragonwyck," she cut in, taking three heavy, waddling steps forward. "My late husband Monty Dragonwyck was a famed highwayman in the waning years of the Victorian era. He was the first highwayman to use an automobile in his work."

From the open doorway came a polite cough. "Begging your pardon, Mrs. Dragonwyck, but the blazing coals are starting to cool, so if you—"

The female mastermind wheeled, quivering. "Bring the brazier in, Salazar," she ordered. "And did you fetch the other interrogation equipment?"

"Yes, ma'am," the man with the exceptionally small nose promptly replied. "I think I ought to mention that the poker is a mite rusty, the heel of the Oregon Boot is slightly lopsided, and the pincers are tarnished."

"Still usable." She returned her attention to Maud. "Now then, dearie, are you ready to tell me about the Marinoff Black Pearls, or shall my underling start getting the poker red hot?"

"I really do not know anything about pearls or what my uncle had to do with them."

Ophelia made another racking throat clearing. "Perhaps a bit of history is in order," she said. "I have been seeking them for quite some time. They are first heard of in the autumn of 1799 when they were given as a gift to Czar Alexander I of Russia by Crown Prince Humbert of Travestania. Just two weeks after he made the gift, he was killed in a small revolution in his own country. Alexander I a few years later gave the pearls to one of his mistresses and she soon succumbed to a severe case of the vapors. The pearls were later stolen, but the man who took them, a minor Russian novelist, was found dead at his desk in the winter of 1813. By this time the pearls had the reputation of being accursed."

"Were I you," said Maud, "I'd steer clear of them."

"All these tales of curses are so much flapdoodle, argle bargle, and balderdash," said the mastermind. "They happen to be worth fifteen thousand pounds. And I mean to have them." She paused. "Now, then, if you don't know where they are, can you tell us where the talking horse is?"

"What does Dobbins have to do with all this?"

"Your late lamented uncle was a partner in some large thefts and burglaries," said Ophelia. "Theo actually tracked down the Marinoff Black Pearls, acquired them in his sly way and brought them to Dr. Bellerman until it was safe to fence them. However, poor Theo was arrested for another crime and locked away."

"Dobbins?"

"Your dear uncle hid the pearls and left a message with the talking horse. If one says 'the Marinoff Pearls' to him, Dobbins will reveal the location."

"How do you know that?"

"Your uncle got a message to Theo. But by the time Theo was finally a free man again, the horse, thanks to you, disappeared."

Maud looked away from the fat woman for a moment. "If I tell you where Dobbins is, there won't be any of this business with hot pokers and other nasty paraphernalia?"

"There would be no need, dearie."

"And I would be free to go?"

"You have my word."

"Well, I'll have to settle for that," the girl said and told the master criminal about the riding stable.

Placing his top-hat on his lap and smoothing his hair yet again, Major Nemo said, "Oy, our quarry is making yet another turn."

"I noticed," said Harry.

The woodlands and the hills beyond brightened and the fog lifted quite a bit. The sky was looking fuzzy, rather than opaque.

A fingerpost at the edge of the latest town they were approaching indicated that the side road the horse wagon was turning onto was leading to the village of Dawlish Wake.

"By Jove," mentioned the little man, "I wonder if that ramshackle castle on yonder hill is where the fat lady is holed up."

Guiding their jitney onto the new road, Harry said, "It does look as though it might suit Ophelia's tastes."

The road quirked to the right and when they next saw the Fellows & Creech wagon, it was parked across the roadway and blocking them.

"Whoa," Harry advised their rented horse, reining up.

From out of the wagon stepped a tall man with a very small nose and well-taken-care-of hunting rifle over his arm. He moved toward them.

The Major very quietly and unobtrusively dropped his Derringer into his hat. "I'll take care of this clunk," he informed Harry without moving his lips.

"Nope, you won't. Let's just—"

Salazar Alhambra halted a few feet away and rearranged his grip on his rifle so that it was aimed directly at Harry. "I believe I'm addressing the noted detective Harry Challenge. I have to tell you that at following, you do not excel. Why, we've been aware of you almost since—"

"You did lead us to Maud, though," said Harry. "And you've also got the talking horse. So from my—"

Nemo, hat in hand, all at once stood up. "You've got a lot of nerve, Buster," he called. "Inflicting that dinky nose of yours on us. Can't you wear a patch over it?"

"Who in the hell are you, you little pipsqueak?"

"Them is fighting words." He flung his top-hat up, caught the small gun in his gloved right hand as it dropped out and went diving off the seat.

"Major!" said Harry.

The midget turned a double somersault as he fell through the air and landed with his highly-polished boots slamming into Salazar's chest.

The tiny-nosed man made an awkward deflating sound and flipped backwards, slapped the road with his back and sent swirls of dust upward. Nemo jumped onto his rifle and forced him to expel it.

Harry, meantime, dropped from the jitney seat, drew his revolver and shot the second lout in the calf as he came running out of the wagon waving a large rusty knife and hollering imprecations.

The shock of the shot caused the heavyset bearded man to pass out. Leaving him in the road, Harry approached the wagon.

✗   ✗   ✗   ✗   ✗

Ophelia Dragonwyck, holding a dainty polka-dot parasol tightly in her gloved fist, was sitting outdoors on a sturdy wicker chair. A small monkey was lolling languidly on her abundant lap.

"Mrs. Dragonwyck," began Maud, who was sitting uneasily on a kitchen chair close beside her on the gray stone porch of the castle, "I have a feeling that—"

"Be still, if you please. Here comes Salazar, a bit late, I must admit, with the horse wagon."

"Salazar is the one with the extremely small nose?"

"It's not at all polite to dwell on the poor man's infirmities." With a grunting display of effort, she was raising herself to an upright position. The monkey dropped, chittering with annoyance.

"My concern is that now that you have Dobbins, you aren't really going to keep your promise about turning me—"

"Do stop nattering," the fat woman suggested in a voice containing some aspects of a growl. "Get on your pretty little feet and come down and confirm that Salazar has the right damned horse."

"Well, he ought to be able to tell a mechanical horse from—"

Tossing the parasol aside, Ophelia began a thumping descent of the thirteen wide stone steps. "Come along, dear girl, come along. I've waited more than long enough for this moment."

The door of the wagon was partially open. A man in a black coat and a floppy slouch hat was sitting half out of the door, looking downcast.

"What in the name of Beelzebub and ninety-nine other fallen angels is wrong with you?" inquired Ophelia as she came thumping up to the wagon.

"It may well be," said Harry, standing up and tipping his black hat. "It may well be the fact that I'm not Salazar Alhambra."

The fat mastermind took two steps closer. "Well, I'll be blowed if it ain't Harry Challenge himself trying to pull the wool over me eyes."

"Very perceptive, ma'am." He had drawn his Colt .38. "Now raise your hands and—"

"Not bloody likely," she roared and made an ambitious leap at him, grabbed him and applied a powerful bear-hug.

Harry's gun fell free as the squeezing intensified. He started concentrating on breathing.

"That's enough of that, you old sow." Major Nemo climbed up over Harry and whapped the aggressive Ophelia on the noggin a few times with a horseshoe. She sighed a bellowing sigh, stumbled backwards, whammed the stones of the courtyard violently and dropped into unconsciousness.

"Thanks, Major." Harry reinstated his breathing.

"Think nothing of it, Challenge." He trotted across the fallen fat woman.

From downhill came the clanging of a police wagon's bells and then the black vehicle rolled up with a supply of uniformed officers and plainclothes Scotland Yard men.

Inspector Beggarstaff disembarked first, handsome and dapper as ever. He paused to relight his pipe. "Ah, Challenge, it looks as though you've beaten me to the target. I thought, indeed, that Scotland Yard's sources of information were impeccable."

Harry grinned politely. "There's Ophelia." He pointed at the supine woman. "This young lady is Maud Bellerman."

She said, "There are still several of Ophelia's minions in that castle, Inspector. Plus Theo Culhane."

"We'll take care of them in a jiffy." He called to the men gathered around the wagon. "Blake, Needham, take six men and search that pile. Hockenberry, get this villainous woman trussed up. Watch out for any sly tricks on her part."

On the top step of the castle a red-bearded man with a rifle emerged. After looking things over, he scurried back inside.

"Now then," the Inspector asked the detective, "what about this missing talking horse?"

"Don't you want to know about the thirteen perfectly-matched Marinoff Black Pearls?" asked Maud.

"Jove, yes. Do you know where they are?"

She smiled. "No, but Dobbins does, apparently." She touched Harry's arm, tilting her head toward the wagon. "He is in there, isn't he?"

"Yep, so let's go in and have a chat with him."

✗   ✗   ✗   ✗   ✗

Maud led Dobbins out of the rear of the wagon and settled him on the stones of the courtyard.

Dobbins was about fifteen hands high, his imitation roan hair was nearly believable and his eyes glowed a faint blue.

He tossed his mane, nuzzled the young woman and said, "Good to see you again, Miss Maud."

Major Nemo pulled at the young woman's skirt. "Introduce me," he requested.

"Patience, Major." Patting the mechanical horse on his nose, she asked, "Dobbins, where are the Marinoff Black Pearls?"

The Inspector slipped his notebook out.

"Oh, sure." The horse's voice was just a bit tinny and when he was speaking, a thin whirring and rattling could be heard somewhere in his hind quarters. "The Marinoff Black Pearls are hidden in the Featherbridge Family Tomb behind the Church of St. Norbert the Divine on the outskirts of London."

"Where exactly?"

'Oh, in the coffin of Sir Nigel Featherbridge (1790–1846)."

"Thank you, Dobbins."

"Say, Miss Maud, when are we—"

She reached up and clicked off the switch at the back of his neck.

"Hey," complained Nemo, "you forgot to tell him you sold him to the Colonel."

She turned away. "Yes, I'll have to do that, Major." She moved close to Harry and took his hand.

Inspector Beggarstaff, after pausing to relight his pipe, offered, "I can escort you to that long-abandoned cemetery, Miss Bellerman."

"That would be helpful," she said.

✗   ✗   ✗   ✗   ✗

Three days later, the view of afternoon London from the large windows of Colonel Bascom's suite at the Imperial-British Hotel showed sunlit thoroughfares and cloudless blue skies.

Major Nemo was saying to Harry, "You're not as bad a gink as I once thought. I'm not especially saddened at the idea that with any luck I'll never encounter you again, but working with you on a detective adventure, I was—"

"Major, please allow me to speak." The Colonel was ensconced in a green Morris chair. "Miss Bellerman turned Dobbins over to us and we are in the process of getting him ready to ship to our native land. He is an exceptional example of technical accomplishment, a harbinger of what lies ahead in the coming years of this grand new century and when he is installed in an honored place in my—"

"Dimwits will pay a nickel to hear him mumble and count to ten." The Major jiggled on his hassock.

The Colonel continued. "I am most exceptionally grateful, Harry, that you brought Dobbins back to me. Here, therefore, is a small bonus check to at least partially express my thanks. And I must add that your capture of that criminal mastermind is also—"

"Give him the blasted check."

Accepting the check, Harry stood and said, "Any time you're in need of exceptional investigative services, call on the Challenge International Detective Agency and—"

"Geez, Harry, you're starting to sound like the old boy."

"Yeah, excuse it, Major."

Colonel Bascom chuckled. "Harry, I have just learned of an exceptionally fine Indian restaurant minutes away from here. The food is superb, the service unique."

"And the prices are impossible," the Major added. "What say, Harry, shall we go out to a fish and chips joint?"

Harry folded the check and slipped it into the breast pocket of his coat. "Gentlemen, I appreciate both of your invitations," he told them. "However, Maud is returning as Tilda Merrydew to the Picadilly Music Hall this evening at eight. And I'm escorting her to a late supper afterwards."

"Ah, a pity you can't join us, but romance is more important."

"Give Maudie a peck on the cheek," advised the Major.

"At the very least," promised Harry as he turned to leave.

✗

Ron Goulart is a prolific science fiction and mystery writer, with over 180 novels to his credit. He is also a noted authority on comic books and comic strips.

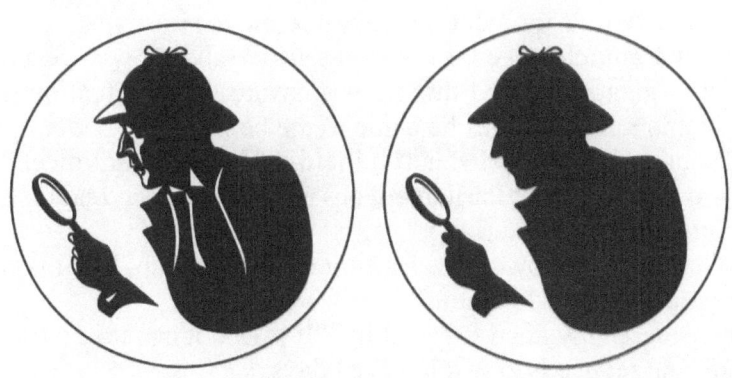

A DEATH IN BALTIMORE

by Arjay Lewis

It was in the summer of 1849 when I found myself requested to appear before the Board of Directors for the British East India Company.

As the second son of a country squire, my brother inherited the family estate, so I found occupation with that famed company. As I was well-bred and properly educated and had served with the British Navy, my duties were those of a ship's captain on excursions to India and China.

The previous two years I remained in London, delegated to office work due to the difficulties my wife Violet suffered in delivering our second son Mycroft. However, with the boy a healthy toddler and my wife recovered from her long bout of child-bed fever, a meeting had been requested to "discuss my position."

So on a hot day in August I arrived in Captain's uniform—which had not been my custom since I'd become an office worker. My hair and beard were trimmed short and I appeared very military in my precision. Promptly at ten in the morning I was escorted into the board room, where a total of five men waited. I removed my hat, placed it under my arm and stood at attention.

They were all dressed in black frock coats and cravats with the exception of Mister Caufield, the head director. He was dressed in a cutaway morning suit with gray and black striped trousers, as well as a gray cravat and vest. He smoked a large cigar and the room wore a slight haze. After a moment he requested me to sit.

Mister Caulfield asked a few pleasantries about my wife's health and I was greatly pleased that he was aware of my situation. However, within a few minutes he came to the heart of the matter.

"Captain Holmes," Mister Caulfield said in his big voice, "I am sure you are aware that Parliament has repealed the Navigation Acts."

"I am, sir. Most disturbing."

"What do you know of the Baltimore Clipper ship?" he asked and placed the cigar into his mouth.

I considered my answer carefully. "It is said it can take a two year journey and reduce it to two hundred days, sir."

This caused a murmur to go through the room. Caulfield went on, "And with the changes in the Acts, American companies can now compete in our trade."

"Yes, sir. There is a common belief that the fresher the tea the better."

Mister Caulfield smiled at my grasp of the circumstances. "Right you are, Captain. These clipper ships give them an advantage."

"If we wish to compete, sir, I would recommend the company invest in several of them—and with all due haste."

"Right you are, right you are!" Mister Caulfield said and then he gave a laugh and turned to the others. "See! Here is a man who understands our predicament."

I looked down at my feet so as not to look too proud in the face of such praise.

"The truth is, sir, we have built such a ship!" Mister Caulfield said. "And we need a captain for the first run."

I shot up from my chair. "And I am your man, sir!" I said perhaps too brazenly. "Where would you have me go? India, China?"

Mister Caulfield chuckled again. "This is why I have called for you, Captain Holmes. Such enthusiasm! But we must choose caution over zeal."

"Sir?"

"I wish for you to test the ship. Press it to its limits and see if we can trust our future to such vessels."

I nodded and returned to my seat. "What would you have me do, sir?"

"I require you to take the ship out in September. You are to pick up cargo in Baltimore, Maryland."

This caused several murmurs about the table.

"America, sir?" I said surprised at what I heard. "You wish me to buy tea from an American company?"

"Indeed, Captain. Then you can set sail to London with a loaded ship. If the vessel performs up to our expectations and with your appraisal, we shall begin construction in earnest!"

So my mission was clear. They wished an experienced captain to take the ship out empty, see how fast it could go, then return fully loaded and yet not risk the trip to the far reaches of China. I surmised as well that going across the Atlantic would be far more of a test than the calmer waters of the Indian Ocean or the Pacific.

So after I made my goodbyes to my sweet Violet, I instructed Sherrinford to keep an eye on his younger brother and his mother and told him that he was "the man of the house." His chest expanded with pride and he gave me a solemn nod that only a five-year-old could muster. I knew the family was in good hands.

We set sail on the ninth of September in fair weather with an experienced crew and a Scotsman, Henry Watson, as my first mate. The crew soon opened the vessel's many sails and we began to move at quite a fast clip indeed. The Americans used the "Baltimore Clipper" since 1845, but this new design carried our vessel at speeds that I was certain would exceed their own.

In spite of several days of poor weather, we were able to arrive in Baltimore harbor by October 3rd, seven days prior to our expected date. We sailed into the harbor at sunset and it was a sight. Many fine ships were in port with the dark water around them. There was the smell of peat and coal fires as an early chill sat heavy in the air.

From the noise and revel I could sense that the streets were filled with displays of public drunkenness. I made inquiries and soon discovered that our arrival corresponded to election day in the city of Baltimore. I learned from the dock-master that many of the polling places were also pubs—called "bars" in the Americas.

Although I had no desire to risk these dirty streets filled with loud men, I had to make contact with the company representative to make arrangements for our shipment earlier than originally planned.

I gave Mister Watson orders that no one was to leave the ship. Then in full uniform and with a pistol hidden in my waistband, I went forth to try to locate our contact, one Charles Morton Stewart, an apprentice with the tea merchant.

Baltimore, I came to discover, was a proponent of gas street lamps, which helped me find my way. As I ventured from the docks, I was approached with numerous entreaties—some quite adamant, that I needed to cast a ballot. This, even though I wore British attire.

At one corner, several large men insisted that I would have to cast a ballot or not be allowed to pass. I moved my coat aside to expose my pistol, which discouraged the ruffians, though they cursed at me as I travelled on. I sought Mister Stewart at his place of business, as well as his home with little success. I found that I wandered the streets no closer to his whereabouts than when I set out.

It was at about eleven at night that I decided it was time to return to the ship. But as I turned a corner outside of a tavern known merely as "Gunner's Hall" I found a man prone on the sidewalk in dismal shape.

I bent to look to him and make sure he was indeed alive. He was dressed in a shabby suit of gabardine with stained and faded pantaloons. He wore a hat that was the brimless tattered remains of what had been a palm leaf straw chapeau.

It was at this point I was joined by an American, who knelt next to me as I sought for the fallen man's breath.

"Good sir," I said to the American, "this man must be taken to a hospital. Will you assist me?"

"Of course, sir. Washington College Hospital is a short distance from here. If we both lift this fellow, we should be able to carry him there."

The pair of us hoisted the fallen gentlemen and my companion guided us through the streets. I found my helper's name was Joseph Walker and he was a typesetter for the local paper.

In but a few minutes we arrived at the hospital. The man awakened and spoke in a faint voice. However, his ramblings made no rational sense.

Once we found a doctor and the man was put abed, I wrote a quick note with my name, my ship and my pier location for the doctors.

I returned to the ship past midnight, to find Watson on deck.

"Mister Watson, I thought you would have retired," I said as I climbed the gangplank.

"I requested first watch out of concern," he responded, his face serious. "Quite a Benjo out there, sir."

"Yes, it is," I said, "but you needn't have worried. I shall go to my berth. See you on the morrow, Mister Watson."

"Sleep well, Cap'n," he said.

As I lay in my berth, I could not help but think about the odd man Mister Walker and I rescued. I also had the queer sensation that he was familiar to me, but I could not place him.

⚔ ⚔ ⚔ ⚔ ⚔

The next day, I went to the merchant's place of business. The streets were empty from the previous evening, the population bent on a return to normalcy or to recover from their overindulgence of the previous day.

Once at the tea merchants, I found Mister Stewart, a man of twenty and one, and showed him my papers of lading. We set about to confirm the order.

"We can load it on the ship earlier than planned, sir," he stated. "But I think I cannot offer to do so until after the Sabbath."

It being merely Thursday, I was surprised at this.

"I cannot have men until Monday, sir? This is quite unacceptable," I said.

"I would offer to do the work myself if it t'would help, but we have a large order that must be completed this Friday and Saturday. Would you have me make the men work on the holy day, sir?"

I shook my head. We arrived a fortnight early and his company's work was planned out. I agreed to this and decided it would be well to offer my crew shore leave so they would be fit for the return voyage.

Because of this turn of events, I was in no haste as I left the Merchant House, so I made my way to the hospital to seek information about my charge.

After I questioned several nurses and described the fellow in detail, I was told to find one Doctor Moran, who was busy in the wards.

It was then a man walked up beside me and said, "*Pardonez-moi,* Monsieur."

I turned to the short, dark-haired man with a thin mustache. He was well-dressed and gentle in his manner.

"Yes, sir?" I said.

"I 'eard you were interested in a man brought in last night? The dark-haired gentleman?"

"Yes, I was the one who found him in the street. Myself and another brought him here."

"And yet—you did not know 'im?" the Frenchman asked, his eyebrows raised.

"He seemed familiar, but I was more concerned for his well-being."

"So you did not know 'e is the writer and poet Edgar Allan Poe?"

I stopped and stared at this gentleman in shock. I was indeed aware of one of Mister Poe's stories called "The Tell-Tale Heart," which I'd read in a magazine by the name of *The Pioneer*. It was a haunting tale and just the memory of it made me shiver involuntarily.

"Is that who it was?" I said. "But what is your connection to that man?"

"My name is C. Auguste Dupin and I am the person Mister Poe came to Baltimore to see."

✗　✗　✗　✗　✗

It was a few minutes later that I sat across from this fellow at a nearby tea shoppe, engrossed in his telling of the unexpected tale.

"I have known Monsieur Poe for over a decade, 'e 'as taken an interest in my pursuits," he said as he gave a sad smile. "'E took several of my cases and wrote them up for the public. Though I have no need for such attention."

"I am familiar with your name, sir. 'The Murders in the Rue Morgue,' 'The Purloined Letter'—yet I always thought those stories were the creation of Mister Poe's restless imagination."

"'E took some—'ow shall I put it—liberties with the work. But Monsieur Poe liked to write of my techniques."

"What brought you here, sir?"

"I came to America for—another purpose, that I cannot reveal. However, I was requested to look into the corruption that is rampant in ze elections by none other than Mister Poe's Cousin Neilson."

"Neilson Poe? What concern are the elections to him?"

"'E is a lawyer and involved in oversight."

I glanced at the many-paned window near our table which looked out upon the streets.

"My ship arrived on election night. I was shocked by the drinking."

"They say it is a custom, but it is 'ard to believe that men choose their representatives while in such a state."

"I walked the streets myself and was confronted by ruffians who ordered me to cast a ballot."

"Even in your uniform?"

"Yes. However, revealing my pistol persuaded them to leave me be."

"I am concerned that Edgar may have been too close to such men. 'E planned to meet with me. I arrived three days ago, but was unable to locate 'im."

"Are you concerned with foul play, sir?"

"Indeed. You were one of ze men who found 'im. I was told 'e was in quite a state."

"Yes. His clothes were a mess and he was unconscious. He woke briefly, but was quite delirious."

Dupin nodded his head. "I visited 'im to today and 'e remains incoherent. I was not able to find out what 'appened. If 'e was captured by such men, they may have plied him with alcohol or drugs."

"Was Mister Poe a drinker, sir?"

"'E tends to have intervals of rampant intoxication followed by long periods of abstinence. 'Owever, since his recent engagement—"

"Mister Poe was engaged?"

"*Mais oui.* 'E was reunited with a childhood sweetheart in Richmond—a widow. When 'e decided to take this step, 'e became a member of the Sons of Temperance."

"What would you advise, sir?"

"I need to recreate the days leading up to 'is misfortune," Dupin said as he rose from his seat and tossed several coins on the table.

"May I assist you, sir?"

Dupin looked me over from head to foot. "If you have other clothes, perhaps something—less military?"

I looked down at my own uniform and gave a nod. "If you can accompany me to my ship, I have more appropriate attire."

We strode out of the tea shoppe and onto the streets. The wind blew a different direction, which brought the stench of the polluted bay to our nostrils.

We ventured on and arrived at my ship in a short time. Monsieur Dupin looked up at the vessel and took my arm to stop my egress.

"This is a most unusual ship," he said in low tones.

"That it is, sir. But I am obligated to say nothing of it."

His eyes moved quickly from stem to stern. "If it can do what I believe it might, it shall change things greatly," he said with an odd smile on his face.

He released me and I marched up the gangplank, gave a nod at the sailor who stood watch and made my way to the officer's quarters.

In the small room reserved for the first mate I found Watson. He held a small board affixed with a paper and held a stump of charcoal in his hand. He saw me and began to rise.

"As you were, Watson," I said, and indicated his work. "What's this, then?"

He turned the board around and there was a well-executed sketch of a nearby lighthouse.

"Well done," I said. "I didn't know you possessed such a talent, Mister Watson."

"I have an interest in lighthouses, sir," he said as he put the drawing aside. "I studied architecture."

My eyebrows went up. "If you studied such, why take the position of First Mate on a ship?"

He smiled. "Aye, and how better to see differing lighthouses, sir?"

A laugh escaped my lips. "Of course." I stepped in from the doorway and lowered my voice. "I must be away from the ship."

"A bit unusual, sir," Watson said.

"I find myself in unusual circumstances. We are not to be loaded until Monday—"

"Monday, sir?"

I gave a nod. "Yes, please arrange shore leave for the men, but also make sure there is a watch on deck for all shifts. That man should have a pistol at all times."

"Are we expectin' trouble, sir?"

"I choose to err on the side of caution. I shall be in civilian clothes and may be difficult to locate. But, be assured I shall return to the ship before the cargo is loaded."

"Aye, sir."

"I apologize if this places a large burden on you, Mister Watson."

"Not at all, sir. If I plan well, I perhaps might have an hour or two on land me-self."

"Good man. Now I must change."

"If I may be so bold, sir, what are ya doing?"

"Assisting in a mystery."

I was dressed in civilian clothes in minutes. I chose some linen that was not as clean as it could be and a coat that I wore when doing labors. I chose an old pair of boots that were scuffed so that I fit in with the common folk in this American city.

I made sure to take my pistol, which I slipped in my belt, as well as a small bag with percussion caps, powder and lead balls.

I walked down the gangplank and Monsieur Dupin looked up at me with a smile.

"Well done, *mon ami*," he said as he looked me over. "You appear quite different."

"I should let you know that I am armed," I said and moved the skirt of my frock coat to reveal the weapon.

He inclined his head. "That may be a wise course, sir."

He turned and began to walk as he headed for another section of the docks.

"We must begin at the beginning," he said as I struggled to catch up to the shorter man's fast gait. "Monsieur Poe arrived at this dock on the 28th of September!"

"Do you know his state of mind?" I said.

"'Is cousins told me that 'e raised funds to start a magazine and just came from seeing 'is betrothed in Richmond."

We arrived at the passenger terminus, if it could even be called that. It was a large wooden structure with one side that opened to train tracks and the other side faced the bay. There were people swarming about, some with small children, others with livestock such as goats or chickens.

"Neilson Poe said they met 'ere," Dupin said as he glanced about.

I took in the structure as people got on and off boats or steamships and stood about to wait for carriages or trains to continue their journey.

"I can't see anything that arouses suspicion."

"I agree, but you must look for what is not obvious," he said, then strode purposefully over to a counter that bore a sign that read "Luggage." He spoke to the man behind the counter who pointed at a small trunk. Dupin nodded gratefully and returned to me.

"What was that about?"

"Neilson said Edgar possessed no luggage when they met. Odd for him, as he was quite fastidious about his apparel."

"So his case is still here?"

"*Oui*, with the chalk marks noting where it was to be unloaded. If 'e 'ad retrieved it, 'e would have wiped away such marks. Come, let us visit Monsieur Neilson Poe, perhaps 'e can reveal a different view."

We left the docks behind and began to walk uphill through the city. Dupin took side streets here and there and soon we stood before a modest home away from the darker parts of Baltimore.

He knocked on the door, which was soon opened by a woman who glared at us.

"May I help you, gentlemen?" she asked as she scowled.

"Madame Poe," Dupin said. "Could I impose to speak to your 'usband?"

"He was up rather late last night."

"I am aware of that, good lady, but please tell 'im Monsieur Dupin is 'ere."

She shut the door without another word and we waited.

"You told me Mister Poe is involved with the elections—" I began.

"'E supervises the elections in the Fourth Ward."

"Where Edgar was found?"

"*Oui.*"

The door opened and before us stood Neilson Poe. Unlike his cousin, he was a robust, heavy-set man whose hair had thinned greatly. He apparently dressed hurriedly and was still buttoning his waistcoat.

"Monsieur Dupin," he said and forced a smile. Then his eye went to me. "Who is this man?"

"'E is one of the men who found your cousin," Dupin said.

Poe drew close to Dupin. "Does he expect a reward?"

"Not at all," Dupin said, "'E wishes to assist in finding out what 'appened."

Poe stood up straight and offered his hand. "Neilson Poe. And you are?"

I took his hand and shook it as I said, "Captain Siger Holmes at your service, sir."

He gazed at me intently. "British? And a sea captain?"

"Both correct, sir," I said as I released his hand.

"Do come in," he said and we followed him into a small parlor, where he bade us sit. "I cannot tell you how upsetting this situation has been—and how much it has cost me," he said as he put on his frock coat and took a large stuffed chair to address us. "As Edgar's only relative in the city, I am afraid his hospital expenses fall to me."

Dupin bowed his head modestly. "I understand, but my concern is for your cousin and my friend."

"As I told you, Monsieur, Edgar left here shortly after I told him what day you would arrive and gave me no indication of where he was going," Poe said. "He did not look well and seemed to be suffering from a headache."

"'E wrote me that he was afflicted with a bout of cholera this summer. That is—if it was indeed cholera."

"He was not looking well, I'll tell you that. I bade him stay, but he claimed no wish to accept my hospitality—quite angrily as I recall."

"Angry, you say?" Dupin asked and leaned back in his chair.

"Yes. Usually my cousin minded his manners, but he was quite out of sorts."

Dupin nodded. "In light of the situation, I must ask if there was animosity towards your cousin?"

"Not from me," Poe said and leaned forward on his knees. "Our disagreements go back years. My wife asked her half-sister Virginia Clemm to stay with us in Baltimore."

"Ah!" Dupin said and raised his index finger. "That woman became Edgar's young wife, am I correct?"

"You are, sir. We both thought that she was too young for Edgar as she was only fourteen at the time. He, however, took this as a plot to prevent her from seeing him and became quite agitated. So Virginia declined our invitation. Edgar married her soon thereafter."

"And she died several years ago," Dupin said.

"Yes, which only made him more angry at me, as if I had anything to do with it. Add to that, five years ago Edgar went through a rough patch. He requested a loan that I was unable to give him, due to my own situation."

"One more question, Monsieur, if you do not mind," Dupin stated simply. "Your cousin owns a cat, is that correct?"

"Yes, it lives in my aunt's house in New York."

"Which is where 'e stays when in that city?"

"Of course. I cannot see what that has to do with any of this."

"And did your cousin claim any other business he wished to accomplish while in Baltimore?"

"He made mention that he had to meet with a literary *provocateur*, but I thought nothing of it," Poe said, almost as an aside.

Dupin's head snapped up. "Did 'e mention a name?"

Poe shook his head. "No, that was all he said."

"You are certain those were 'is exact words?" Dupin said, a sparkle in his eye.

"I believe so, yes."

"So Edgar's intention was to assist you, sir?" I said to Dupin.

Dupin looked over at me and nodded. "'E wished once again to study my techniques of ratiocination."

"Your talents were quite fruitful," Mister Poe said and turned to me as he pointed at Dupin. "This man was able to find the leader of a gang of ruffians when no one else could!"

Dupin leaned back in his chair and stared up at the ceiling. "The fellow goes by the name 'Passano,' which is similar to the Italian word for 'countryman.' 'E leads a group 'oo call themselves ze 'Pug-Uglies.'"

Poe turned to me. "We were able to limit their operations in 'cooping' quite severely. This may have been the most legitimate election in years and the Whigs took it on the chin."

"Cooping?" I said. "What is that?"

Dupin nodded. "These gangs take people off the street, ply zem with liquor."

Mister Poe continued. "They keep them in a room known as a 'coop' and force them to vote again and again, often dressing them in different clothing to fool the election officials."

I nodded. "This could explain what happened to Edgar. His garb was stained and ill-fitting."

"My cousin would not go out in unflattering attire," Poe said.

"If Edgar was aware of what you were doing, Monsieur Dupin," I said, "perhaps he attempted to investigate on his own and was encumbered by the very men of which you speak."

Dupin rose from his chair. "I 'ave other conjecture as well. But we must go to the place 'e was found before I may construct an opinion respecting my friend's misfortunes."

Mister Poe and I rose as well. "God speed to you, sir," Mister Poe said. "I shall go visit my cousin at the hospital and see if he has been released from his delirium."

All three of us made for the door and were outside to observe the sun was now well past its zenith. Dupin and I went off in one direction and Neilson Poe another. Dupin seemed lost in thought as we wandered on and took several turns. I endeavored to keep up and found my mind wandered as we travelled the dirty cobblestone sidewalks and pressed-earth streets.

Dupin turned to me and said, "I am sure 'e will keep the ship safe."

"Yes, so am I," I replied unwittingly and then abruptly stopped and stared at my companion, who came to a halt as well.

"Dupin," said I, gravely, "how was it possible you should know I was concerned with my ship?"

"You were not. You were concerned that your first mate was not up to the task of protecting it."

My mouth fell open and Dupin looked positively amused.

"Do not be so surprised, *mon ami*," Dupin said and began to walk again. "I will explain that you may comprehend all. As we walked I saw your eye light upon a ship's model in the window of a house as we passed and then your brow furrowed in concern. This led your thoughts to your first mate and that fact that you 'ave been entrusted with a ship which is new and unique. You felt torn in your duty and your curiosity over Monsieur Poe's dilemma."

"I do not hesitate to say that I am amazed," I said as I caught up to him.

"It is merely observation and deduction. For me, this is very simple," he said with a shrug.

"Elementary, you might say?"

"Indeed. Now I have a puzzle for you."

"What is that, sir?"

"What do cholera, a cat, and a literary agent 'ave in common to our friend's plight?"

I paused and considered this odd statement. "I certainly have no idea, sir. Do you?"

"Not at this precise moment, but it is by these deviations from the plane of the ordinary that reason feels its way in search for the truth."

We had now arrived in the center of the business district a block or two from the docks. There were men in frock coats and top hats milling about. On the corners sat beggars in rags and nearby a woman with several children pleading for assistance.

We reached a large structure with the words "Exchange Building" carved into the stone. Monsieur Dupin took me quickly up to a small office on the second floor. Painted upon the glass door was the name "American Telegraph."

"Wait here, I will be but a moment," he said as he went in.

Through the glass I could see men moving about and was curious of the purpose of this visit. In England, telegraphic communication was established along the train lines and it was possible to send messages from place to place and even person to person. However, I was not aware of how extensive this communication might be in the New World.

Dupin soon came out and we set off in earnest.

"Are we going to pursue this Passano fellow?" I asked.

"With your indulgence, I am examining several lines of inquiry."

We walked on until we reached Gunner's Hall, the very place I discovered Poe the previous evening.

"Could you tell me 'ow you found 'im?"

"He was lying upon the sidewalk," I said and moved to the position, a nearby lamp-post acting as a guide. "It was at this very spot."

Once again Dupin crouched low and examined the place I pointed to with rapt attention, his eyes going over every detail as if to affix it in his memory.

He soon rose and we walked into the pub behind us. I carefully avoided the spittoons as our feet pushed through the sawdust that littered the floor.

Monsieur Dupin walked up to the bar and requested a beer. I gave a nod and the pub landlord drew me a pint as well.

"Much excitement yesterday," Dupin said to the landlord, who merely gave a shrug as he took our copper coins.

"Yeah, it all beat the Dutch if you ask me," he said. He was a lanky man with a bad eye that stared off and a mouthful of crooked teeth.

"I heard a gentleman was found on the sidewalk," I said as I sought to get information from the man.

"T'ain't election night if we don't have a body or two on the side-walk. Last year a bad egg got into a fight, and pulls out an Arkansas toothpick—"

We both stared at the man dumbfounded.

He could sense our confusion. "That's a knife about—yea big—" He demonstrated the length with his hands. "Both of 'em got cut up, I'll tell you that."

"Our concern is for ze man last night," Dupin said. "'E is a companion of ours."

"We would appreciate anything you can tell us," I said.

"I don't care beans what takes place here on election day. Lots of folk come from out of town." He leaned closer, "But, I'll tell you this. That fellow was staying here for the last few days. Him and his friends."

"He stayed here?" I said a frown on my face.

The man nodded. "In the upstairs room. His friend paid for it. He came down a couple times but din't look well and acted all possessed."

"He was behaving erratically?" I wondered.

"Yep. And the two fellows who was with him, well, one acted like he was the biggest toad in the puddle. And the other fellow called him—get this—the Grand Turk."

"Was zat the very words? It is important," Dupin said.

"Yep. They met the fellow here—what—six days ago. Got themselves on a fine bender—that's all I know."

"Can you tell me anything else about 'is companions?" Dupin inquired, his face pallid. "It might be a matter of life and death!"

The landlord looked at Dupin curiously. "One was average height, beard, no 'stache. The other had curly hair, spectacles. They bought a bottle of whiskey each day. I remember the 'Turk' man because I figured from the way he talked, he was from New York."

Dupin leapt up at this. "It is as I surmised! Thank you, good sir."

Dupin tossed a pair of silver coins on the bar and with his drink only partially consumed, made for the door. I was quick on his heels.

"I must go to Edgar, but I fear it is too late," he said.

"Can I help?"

"*Oui*, you can, *mon ami*," he said and stopped. "Please return to your ship. I must make inquiries. If zey are fruitful, I will need your assistance on the morrow."

"Is there nothing more I can do?" I said.

"If what I believe is true, there is little that can be done for Edgar. I shall call upon you in ze morning," Dupin turned and set off.

I was confused by this turn of events, but made my way back to the ship.

I arrived at the dock and began my climb up the gangplank.

"Halt, 'oo goes there?" came a voice I recognized as my Helmsman, a man named Harris.

"'Tis the Captain," I replied, and in the darkness I saw his arm which held a pistol, lower.

"Sorry, sir, didn't recognize you in the dark."

"It's fine, Harris. Are you on first watch?"

"'Till six bells, sir."

"Allow me to get into uniform and I shall relieve you. You may go to the pub if you wish."

I was now on the ship and I could see him smile in the light of the half-moon.

"That would be fine, sir, if you've a mind to."

"I need to clear my head and standing out on deck in the night air would help."

I excused myself and went to my cabin where I quickly got on my double-breasted tailcoat and proper attire.

I returned to the deck, whereupon Harris gave me his pistol. "Be back on ship by eight bells," I directed.

He nodded. "I will for sure, sir, thank you, sir" he said as he retreated down the gangplank.

I looked up at the lights of the city. Baltimore by night was a series of lit windows, some that merely had candlelight or oil lantern, while others enjoyed the luxury of gas lighting. The gaslit street lamps cast a ghostly glow, which created pools of light and darkness. Further away in the poorer section of the city, the windows and the streets were quite dark.

I looked up into the starlit night and puzzled what Dupin discovered that told him there was little hope for Mister Edgar Allan Poe.

⚔ ⚔ ⚔ ⚔ ⚔

The next morning, as I had breakfast and tea, our ship received a visit from none other than young Mister Stewart, who was ushered into my cabin by Mister Watson.

"Good morning, Captain," he said as I rose from my chair to greet him.

"May I offer you anything, Mister Stewart?" I asked.

"No, nothing at all. I come with good news. Our schedule has been altered so we may load your cargo this very day."

It was the Friday, three days ahead of the original plan.

"That will suit me well, sir, and please my superiors," I said.

He gave a nod. "I shall have my men bring the cart and start loading."

He soon took his leave. I went to Mister Watson and gave him the news, which he took well.

"If we can make as good time on our return voyage, we'll be back in England by early November," he said.

"Yes, quite amazing. But I must solve a difficult puzzle this very day, which may require my full attention. Can you manage without me?"

"Easily, sir. The crew is here and between their men and ours we shall load the cargo this very day."

I quickly returned to my cabin and changed into my worn civilian clothes of the previous day to travel with Monsieur Dupin once again. My timing was impeccable, for as soon as I was dressed Mister Watson announced that "a Frenchman wishes to see you, sir."

I welcomed Dupin in and offered him tea, which he accepted gratefully. He wore the same clothes as the previous day, and appeared a bit tired from his excursions.

"Have you learned of what happened to Mister Poe?" I asked as he sipped his tea.

"*Oui*, and it is most terrible. I was correct that there is little that can be done. My friend will not last for more than a day or two."

"That is sad news, indeed."

"'Owever, with your 'elp, I may be able to find justice or at least let the villain responsible know that I am aware of 'im."

"In any way I can be of service, sir."

"Fine," he said and finished his tea. "Then bring your pistol, I 'ave a coach waiting."

I slipped my weapon into my trousers and we went down the gangplank to the waiting hansom.

"I'm aggrieved to hear about Mister Poe," I said as the carriage wended its way through the streets.

"It is a pity that I must leave and cannot be by 'is bedside. I was brought over to America for a task in ze nation's capital."

"Whatever for?"

"I am not at liberty to discuss it. 'Owever, I believe there is a plot against the American president."

I looked at my companion and realized that there was much more to the man than I knew.

Soon we arrived at the corner of Fayette and Calvert Streets, where a building stood with a simple sign that read, "City Hotel."

Dupin gave the driver a few coins and we stepped out. He bounded up the stairs of the front stoop and was met by a gentleman.

"Is 'e 'ere?" Dupin asked and the gentleman nodded his assent. "Monsieur Holmes, this is Monsieur McLaughlin, ze proprietor."

"One of the proprietors," the man said. "If you wish to speak to the gentleman, he is in room ten, but intends to leave soon."

Dupin turned to me, "Come, we must go."

We quickly walked up the flight of stairs and knocked upon the numbered door.

"Who is it?" came in reply to our summons.

"Two men 'oo desperately need to speak with you," Dupin said.

The door was pulled open and there before us stood a man with a high forehead and a chin beard, but not the traditional mustache that might have accompanied it.

"What is the meaning of this?" the man demanded. I could see on the bed a small trunk that he apparently had been packing.

"Murder, monsieur," Dupin said with an angry look on his face. "I suggest you speak with us."

"And if I refuse?" the man growled.

I pulled my frock coat aside to reveal my pistol, whereupon the man gasped and took several steps back. Dupin and I stepped in and quietly shut the door behind us.

"I am a mere author—" the man began, but Dupin raised his hand to silence him.

"I 'ave put the problem together within my mind," Dupin said. "I know what you 'ave done."

The man sputtered and looked from me to Dupin. "I have no idea who you are—"

"Then, I will 'elp you. We are friends of Edgar Allan Poe. Ze man you 'ave murdered!"

The fellow's mouth moved but nothing came out.

"I will tell you 'ow I know this, Monsieur," Dupin said and began to pace. "I recommend you sit down."

The man lowered himself into a chair.

"This was a plot you began perhaps even a year ago and you came 'ere to make sure it played out to your expectations."

"I have no idea—" the man said.

"You say you are an author? You are in fact a literary *provocateur*. You assemble books of poetry from the works of many far more qualified than you, including Monsieur Poe."

The man looked angrily from Dupin to me. "I still don't see—"

"Then I shall improve your vision!" Dupin said loudly. "Rabies."

The man grew pale and closed his mouth, all his bluster gone.

"You are familiar, *oui*? An incurable disease that is always fatal. That is why I am 'ere."

The man frowned.

"Let me walk you through what I believe you did. At some previous time, you abducted Monsieur Poe's pet cat, am I correct, sir?

The man stared at Dupin in disbelief.

"You kept it for a day or two in a cage with another animal, *n'est pas*? An infected animal."

The man's mouth became a tight line.

"Whereupon, you returned the cat to Monsieur Poe, who doted and played with the animal, unaware that it was now rabid. I know this, as I 'ave contacted 'is aunt. Ze cat is quite sick as well."

The man looked from Dupin to the door, which was blocked by me.

"It took time for the infection to affect Monsieur Poe. 'Owever, you were told by 'is aunt, Mrs. Clemm, that 'e 'ad a bout of cholera this summer. You knew better and were certain ze condition 'ad taken 'old."

My hand went to my weapon, a move which was not lost on our prisoner.

"You 'ad to be sure. So, once you knew 'e came to Baltimore, you arrived ahead of time to waylay 'im."

"This is ridiculous—" he protested.

"I would have thought so as well if not for the fact that Monsieur Poe and your companion said your name."

The man rose and I slipped my pistol from my belt.

"What?" was all he could manage.

"Ze man with you was overheard as he called you the 'Grand Turk,' a nickname you are known by in New York. I assume it was Charles

Hoffman, a writer acquaintance of yours, 'oo lives in Washington. I am sure he has already returned there."

He began to sweat quite profusely.

"I also visited Edgar last night. Ze nurses claimed he said 'Reynolds' while in delirium. But to me, it was clear 'e was saying 'Rufus.' That is your name, is it not? Rufus Wilmot Griswold?"

Griswold looked again from me to Dupin. "This is the most spurious—"

"Non, monsieur, it is not. You and Monsieur Poe had a deep animosity going back years. You both 'ave exchanged literary barbs on the magazines you both 'ave written and edited."

Dupin moved to a nearby dresser and leaned upon it.

"Did 'e know 'ow you have visited 'is aunt, built a relationship where you pretended to be a devotee of your foe's work?"

"I am an admirer!" Griswold said and stepped away from the chair. "He is a greater writer than I shall ever be. But the man insulted me, again and again—"

"So you took matters into your own 'ands."

"I have done nothing! I came here to discuss a collection of his works, nothing more."

"You kept him locked away at that tavern for days. Plied him with alcohol and watched 'im deteriorate. I am sure Monsieur Hoffman thought you were there merely 'ere to show Edgar a fine time and mistook Edgar's wild delusions as the result of drink."

Griswold showed surprise that Dupin knew this, but he quickly calmed himself. "You have no verification of any of this. I came here to discuss business. Mister Poe is in the hospital, so my business is concluded."

"It was after Monsieur Hoffman took leave. You knew of the custom of 'cooping' and you dressed Edgar in clothes not 'is own and left 'im out on the street to be dismissed as a mere drunk."

"He was a drunk—as well as a drug user," Griswold said haughtily. "If he dies—"

"And you know 'e will—"

"Then it is by his own hand. If the cat is infected, any animal could have done it, it is common enough," Griswold said as a smile crept onto his face.

"I would not smile so, villain," I said and looked down upon the shorter man who backed away from me.

He turned to Dupin. "I know who you are, Monsieur Dupin, and I am aware of your techniques. But this is mere conjecture, which does not take the place of documentation and attestations. There is neither witness nor proof of any crime."

"You are correct, sir," Dupin said. "But you now 'ave the knowledge that I know the truth and I will be watching you."

"Watch as you wish," Griswold said and turned to his luggage. "I will ask you gentlemen to leave my room or must I call for a constable and press charges against you for confining me?"

I wished strongly to take away the man's smug look with the back of my hand. However Dupin, as if reading my mind again, took my arm and said, "We shall go. But what you have done is most wicked, indeed, as you are in the position to publish Monsieur Poe's works"

"What?" Griswold said, startled. "How could you know—"

Dupin stepped close to the man. "That Edgar's will names you 'is literary executor? *Oui*, I know. I am sure ze aunt told you. I believe it was then that this plot formed within your mind."

The look of shock faded and Griswold began to smile again.

I have never had such a strong desire to put a bullet between a man's eyes as I did at that moment.

"We shall bid you *adieu*, but believe me when I tell you that at some point, Monsieur, you will pay for this," Dupin said, opened the door and we walked out.

Soon we stood out on the street again and walked wearily back towards the docks.

"How did you find out all this?" I asked as we trudged slowly.

"It is simple. I was aware of the ongoing problems Edgar had with Monsieur Griswold. When Neilson Poe said a literary *provocateur*, I knew that was Edgar's pet name for Griswold. Also, I realized some of the stages of rabies could resemble cholera. 'Ow could 'e 'ave gotten it? Only by 'is pet cat. So when we went to the telegraph office, I sent two telegrams. One to Mrs. Clemm to ask about the cat and if she'd had any visitors. She telegraphed back that Monsieur Griswold visited 'er often when Edgar was out of town and that Edgar's cat was near death."

"So he was ingratiating himself with the woman, I suppose."

"*Oui*. Ze other telegram went to Monsieur Griswold's office to ask if 'e was in New York."

"Which he was not."

"Correct. Add to that, when we spoke to the barkeep last evening and he said the man called his companion the 'Grand Turk.' That is a nickname Griswold is known by. When I visited Edgar last evening, I examined 'is arms and found what 'ad been a rather nasty cat bite, old, but still visible on 'is forearm. I zen realized that Monsieur Poe's delirium was the same as the final stages of rabies, of which there is no cure."

"And he spoke the man's name."

"Once I knew 'e was saying Rufus, the final piece fell into place. Then it was merely a matter of locating the 'otel the man was staying, which I did before I came to you this morning."

"How are you so familiar with diseases?"

"I have many interests. I have a friend, a young professor 'oo has taught me much. I expect great things from 'im in the future. 'Is name is Louis Pasteur and rabies is one of 'is pursuits."

"So there is nothing we can do for Edgar?"

Dupin shook his head sadly. "All that is left is to say my goodbyes and wait for the inevitable."

We approached my ship, which was busy with men as they unloaded burlap bags from a large horse-drawn cart which were then carried aboard.

"Ah," Dupin said. "Your cargo. Tea is it not?"

"Yes," I said.

He smiled at this. "A British ship buying tea in America? What a curious idea."

"Perhaps."

"A test of the craft's design?"

I smiled. "Like you, Monsieur, I am not liberty to discuss it."

I handed Dupin one of my calling cards. "If I can ever be of assistance again, please contact me."

He sighed as he took the card. "It is a pity that we 'ad such a poor result."

"I must agree. That smug fellow succeeded at murder and we have no way to prosecute him for the crime—it galls me."

"Still the idea of using a disease as a weapon," Dupin said, as his hand rubbed his chin. "It is an interesting concept."

"A horrifying one," I said as I offered my hand. "Monsieur, it has been an honor."

Dupin took it and gave it a hearty shake. "It 'as been an honor for me as well."

Without another word Dupin walked away and I boarded my ship, put on my uniform and supervised the cargo with Watson. We would set sail the next morning at first light.

✗　✗　✗　✗　✗

Monsieur Dupin did contact me over the ensuing years and I became quite familiar with his amazing techniques, which on occasion I have demonstrated to my sons.

I also kept myself familiar with Mister Griswold as well as I could. The villain did put out collections of Mister Poe's writings and profited from his rival's demise.

It was not until 1857, a full eight years later, that I read of Mister Griswold's sudden passing from tuberculous.

The only odd thing was that his family stated he received a visit from an unknown Frenchman soon before he took to bed.

I wondered if Monsieur Dupin had finally taken vengeance for his friend and dealt out justice for the one case he could not bring to the authorities.

I would never be sure.

✗

Arjay Lewis, performer, actor and award-winning writer. He had over 10 published books, and his novel *The Muse: A Novel of Unrelenting Terror*, has won 14 awards in the Horror category. He also is the author of the *In The Mind* series, which consists of seven novels with more to come.

JEWELS IN THE SUN

by Laird Long

Margaret Palmer parked the car in front of the Ferguson's house and turned to her colleague.

"Keep your eyes and ears and mind open," she advised the young man. "And let me do the talking. I've got thirty-years experience handling claims like these. And you've got… a lot to learn."

"You think the Ferguson's jewellery wasn't really stolen from that Caribbean resort?" Cory McNeil responded eagerly. "That maybe they're trying to finance their vacation with the $30,000 insurance payout? Or maybe they ran up some big gambling losses at the casinos down there, and need the insurance money to pay off those debts?"

"I'm not saying anything—yet," Margaret cautioned. "Keep in mind, though, most claims *aren't* fraudulent. But we'll find out. And remember, questioning clients requires tact. So watch and listen and learn."

The two claims adjusters exited the car and walked up to the front door of the Ferguson's home. Cory punched the bell.

Charmaine Ferguson opened the door. The woman was wearing a sleeveless yellow sundress, despite the chilly temperatures outdoors.

Margaret greeted her client warmly, shaking Charmaine's extended hand. "Good heavens!" she exclaimed, taking the woman's other hand in hers and admiring Charmaine's bare, brown arms and hands. "You can certainly tell *you've* been out in the sun someplace hot. You're positively bronzed!"

Charmaine beamed.

"Not a tan line anywhere, huh, Mrs. Ferguson?" Cory said, grinning as he looked the woman over. "That *we* can see, anyway. Your husband might say different, though, huh?"

Margaret grimaced and released Charmaine's hands as Joe Ferguson, Charmaine's husband, appeared in the doorway.

Charmaine's smile flickered and went out. "We *did* have a lovely two weeks on the islands," she said to Margaret, "until the last night—when my watch and two rings were stolen."

Margaret nodded sympathetically. "That was certainly unfortunate, yes. May we come in for a moment?" She cast a sidelong glance at her colleague. "*I* just have a few questions to ask, if that's all right?"

"Sure," Joe said. "No problem."

Once seated in the Ferguson's living room, Margaret gestured at Cory. The young man fumbled a claims file out of his briefcase and handed it to his boss.

She glanced at its contents, then said, "According to the report you filed with the local police, your two diamond rings and your platinum watch were taken from your hotel room sometime during the final night of your two-week stay when you were sleeping."

"That's right," Charmaine said. "I took them off before I went to bed—as I always do—and put them in the drawer of the nightstand next to the bed. And when we woke up in the morning, they were gone."

"We didn't hear anybody break into our hotel room, Margaret," Joe added. "Like we told the police just before we left—we had a plane to catch, you see—Charmaine and I were both very tired, and we're both sound sleepers."

Margaret was about to follow-up. But Cory interjected, "Did you wear the rings on your left hand, Mrs. Ferguson? The watch, too?"

"Well, yes, of course," Charmaine replied. "Where else would a woman wear her wedding rings?"

Margaret nodded. "There's no chance you could have lost them—on the beach, say?"

"Not a chance," Joe answered. "Charmaine never took them off expect right before bed."

"I don't swim, you see, Margaret," the woman added. "I—we—*did* spend a lot of time on the beach, of course, but I wasn't foolish enough to take off my jewellery and leave it lying around there, with all the people around."

"Did you gamble a lot at the casinos?" Cory brashly asked.

Charmaine and Joe frowned.

Margaret hastily said, "What my colleague means to say, is—"

"I think you two filed a false claim in an effort to defraud the insurance company," Cory finished the sentence off for his boss.

All three of the others gaped at the insurance man. As he followed-up calmly, "If Mrs. Ferguson was out on the beach under the hot sun for two weeks, with her rings and watch on her fingers and wrist—as she 'claims'—then she should have some very visible tan lines on her left hand and wrist. Which she doesn't."

Margaret Palmer smiled proudly. Joe and Charmaine Ferguson burned.

✗

Laird Long: Big guy, sense of humor; pounds out fiction in all genres. Has appeared in many anthologies and mystery magazines and resides in Winnipeg, Canada.

THE UNEXPECTED

by J.P. Seewald

"You are our prisoner, Señor. If you do not cooperate and do just as we tell you then your friends will not find much left after the piranhas finish picking your bones clean."

The blindfold was removed from his eyes, but there was little to see. A stygian darkness surrounded him. He blinked several times and tried to adjust his sight. He'd been bound, blindfolded and gagged at the time of the kidnapping and during the long ride. At first he'd been knocked unconscious.

Later, returning to his senses, he felt the bumpy ride, even in the limousine. The automobile had become his prison, a place of confinement. He considered how such a fine car generally represented wealth and symbolized worldly success. Ironically, for him, it had become a place of fear and incarceration. Claustrophobia set in. He told himself not to panic—he did his best not to panic. But the terror seized him like a pit bull clamping its jaws around the throat of a poodle.

Now they pushed him forward into the night. It had been growing dark when they cut his driver's throat, threw the man from the car and then took him prisoner. He realized time had passed but wasn't certain how much. He'd been stripped of his phone. It was pitch black, no moon or stars overhead. However, the unmistakable sounds and smells of the jungle saturated his consciousness. He felt his shirt soak through. His sweat stank of fear.

"Who are you? What do you want with me?"

There was the flick of light. He saw his captor clearly now. Sharp white teeth smiled at him, but there was no warmth to the smile. This was the man who killed the driver. He felt a chill slither down his spine and palpable pain in his stomach.

"I am called Diego. There are those who prefer El Diablo." Not without reason. The nickname fit.

Diego was short, of a swarthy complexion, with small black eyes that glittered unnaturally, darting about under thick bushy black brows. He sensed the smaller man's energy and had another disturbing, unsettling thought. Diego had the look of a fanatic, a terrorist, a madman.

"Soon, Mr. Saunders, you will be honored by the presence of our leader."

"You've made a mistake. Let me go." His mouth felt dry.

"What will you offer me in return? Gold and riches? Perhaps you would sell me your very soul?" Diego offered a twisted smile.

The American shook his head, unable to speak. He shuddered involuntarily.

The rope used to bind his hands was painfully cutting off his circulation. He tried to move his numb fingers around but was discouraged by the savage expression on Diego's face. Fear gnawed at him like a hungry rat. The American tried to maintain a calm demeanor by reassuring himself that he was secure in his position with the company. They wouldn't let anything happen to him—would they?

The two men brought him into an old building of some sort. Diego's cohort lit candles, giving the place a form of distorted illumination.

"This was once a warehouse," Diego said. "A *grande* owned the entire plantation. It is nothing but a ruin now. So greatness lives and dies. Are you a man of much pride I wonder?" Diego smiled at him again. Those white teeth looked sharper than ever, like a chainsaw that could cut through just about anything.

Another man entered the warehouse. He was much taller than Diego or any of the other men who followed behind him. The broad powerful chest was reminiscent of a Kodiak bear. He moved with authority and confidence in his khaki uniform. Those around him brandished automatic weapons, rifles and sub-machine guns. Obviously, this was Estaban, the leader of the revolutionaries.

"I have captured him for you," Diego said to the big man. "Here is Rowland Saunders, the company's executive vice-president." Diego smiled in a toothy, self-satisfied manner. Such teeth were blinding in the darkly illuminated room. He looked like a well-fed panther.

Estaban stared at the American, cocking his head to one side in an appraising manner. "You are younger than I expected." The voice was deep, rumbling.

"And your English is very good."

Estaban accepted the compliment with a patrician nod of his head.

"Why have I been kidnapped?" God, his mouth was dry!

"Why do you think?" Estaban, for all his revolutionary fervor, seemed a careful man with words.

"You want a ransom?"

"Naturally that is part of it."

"I am not rich," he said.

Estaban shrugged. "Mr. Saunders, we are not interested in mere money. We require the release of certain political prisoners. They are victims of the current regime."

"Why was the limousine driver killed? His death was unnecessary."

Estaban turned to Diego. "How do you answer the American's accusation?"

"It needs no answer," Diego sputtered. "Ask Juan. The man resisted us."

"You have your answer," Estaban said, dismissing the matter with a wave of one large callused hand. "We fight a war of liberation. In war, people die. Many of our people have been imprisoned unjustly by the military junta. Their sole crime was to dissent, to disagree with the brutal practices of the existing regime. For this they were tortured and murdered."

"I sympathize," he said in a controlled voice.

"Do you? Is there compassion in your heart or ice in your veins?"

Careful, he warned himself, handle this guy like the detonator on a bomb. "Americans try to support the forces of democracy and justice everywhere in the world, but we don't approve of acts of terrorism under any circumstances."

Diego spat in his face. The warm wetness caught him on the cheek and offered a sharp contrast to Diego's cold contempt.

"*Embustero!*" Diego's insult exploded in his face like a grenade.

"Enough," Estaban commanded. "Mr. Saunders, you will write a message to your company for us. This letter will state the terms by which you will be returned to them. No doubt since you are a man of wealth and importance, they will be eager to make payment."

"What if they can't secure the release of your friends?"

"Let us hope for your sake they are able, otherwise…"

"I know. My bones will glisten in the sun."

Diego smiled at him, his sharp teeth shining like fine porcelain. "No, *Señor*, the piranhas, they don't leave even the bones." That had to be a lie, but it still managed to freeze his marrow. His heart pounded like a racehorse on the final furlong. Again fear caused visceral pain. It was all he could do not to double over in agony, assaulted by terror.

He had to keep calm. Taking a few deep breaths, he looked around the old primitive warehouse. What had been kept here? Sugar cane, bananas?

As for Estaban, he mentally determined to cut the big man down to size. He studied the high cheekbones that marked the leader as part Indian, but Estaban also had the arrogance of the conquistadors. The massive muscular frame and mocha skin suggested African lineage as well. Whatever heritage Estaban had, he was an intimidating man, a force to be reckoned with. He sensed that Estaban's intellect, though not well-schooled, was every bit as keen as his own.

He saw this situation almost as a game, a challenge and test of his survival abilities. He tried to imagine his captor naked, lost in the jungle, prey to every treacherous peril. Who was Estaban, anyway? Just another man, a mortal being like himself. He tried hard to forget that Estaban held the power of life and death over him.

Another man entered the room. He immediately recognized him as the kidnapper who put a gun to his head. The recollection made him shudder and his stomach sicken. The memory of Diego slashing the driver's throat flooded over his consciousness like a river.

Estaban turned to the man he called Juan and they conversed together in a rapid, excited flow of Spanish. Although the American prided himself on his facility for languages, he could not understand much of what was being said. But he could see Estaban growing angry, his color deepening. Then he turned furiously on Diego. His eyes flashed with immense fury. Estaban was cursing profusely. He understood that well enough. There was total silence in the warehouse as everyone watched and listened.

Finally, Estaban turned and spoke to the American. "You have not been truthful with us. You are not Rowland Saunders. Juan informs me that one of our people has seen Mr. Saunders sitting in his corporate office comfortably smoking Cuban cigars. He is described as middle-aged and fat. Who are you and what were you doing in Mr. Saunder's car?"

He could scarcely breathe. "I am a member of the company, but I'm not important like Mr. Saunders. I might be someday. Right now, I'm just an errand boy, a messenger."

Estaban turned an accusing look toward Diego.

"But he was in the back seat of the big automobile!"

"I was sent to Mr. Saunders's home to deliver some reports he'd requested. He was having his driver take me back to the office."

"Surely they will pay for his return!" Diego said.

"No, I very much doubt that," he said. "Not all Americans are rich. I am not."

"You have family," Diego persisted.

"No, I am an orphan." That was true enough. He'd spent his childhood in a series of foster homes, unloved and unwelcome. But he did not pity himself. It had taught him not to rely on other people. He'd learned instead to study them, to determine their weaknesses. He already knew that Estaban's source of vulnerability was his enormous ego.

He realized that causing Estaban to believe he was expendable was taking an enormous risk. But it was a gamble that could work to his advantage—at least he hoped so.

"Let us kill him," Diego shouted, his voice raw, savage. "I will take pleasure in his death. *Muerte!*" the personification of death cried out, shaking his fist in a menacing manner.

"I agree," Estaban said with steady intent, "there must be a death, a lesson taught. But let the man who deserves to suffer be the one to die. Let all know Estaban is a just man." Estaban signaled Juan, pointing a long lean finger at Diego. "It is your mistake. You are in the wrong."

The small dark eyes opened wide in disbelief. Diego screamed his rage as they dragged him from the room. Estaban's chin jutted out and his lower lip was set in granite. "Fools and blunderers have no place with me."

The leader now fixed his gaze on the American. "Now what shall I do about you?"

"Let me go. That would be the sensible thing and you are very wise." He hoped this appeal to the man's vanity would work.

"Why should I make such a decision?" Estaban did not seem convinced.

"A man of your insight, I'm certain you are aware that if I were quietly returned, the incident would be forgotten. If, on the other hand, I were to disappear permanently, you would lose respect among the very people whose support you seek. Return me and I will always remember I owe you my life. I will return the favor someday. I swear it. I will not always be unimportant."

Estaban laughed, a deep-chested show of amusement. "The fable of the lion and the mouse?"

"Exactly."

"You are most persuasive, but then we all know a man will promise anything to save his own life."

"*Muerte!*" someone called out. Others took up the chant.

His stomach was a vortex of nausea. Fortunately, Estaban silenced them. Estaban ordered the American to follow him. His legs were like sponges. It took great effort to move into the small separate room. The leader waved his followers away as one would swat at flies, then firmly shut the archaic door behind them.

"We will speak in English. None of them understands your language very well, but it is best to be cautious. Infiltrators can be cleverer." Estaban removed a revolver from the holster at his hip and placed it against the American's forehead.

The atmosphere in the tiny room was suffocating, the air thick as split pea soup. Perspiration trickled down his armpits. Fear seized his throat like an attack dog's teeth. A wave of pain tore through him stomach, which he clenched, doing his best not to throw up and humiliate himself.

"Do not misunderstand me, my American friend, I am truly grateful. I had a problem. Now it is solved. Everyone thinks you were kidnapped by mistake. They will never know that Diego was deliberately misinformed."

He stared at Estaban in disbelief. "I don't understand why you'd want to get rid of him. He seemed completely loyal."

"Perhaps too loyal. He is or was my second in command. Ambition does strange things to men's appetites and Diego has known much hunger. I had begun to see the evil in him. He was not to be trusted. He was a danger to me."

"You can put that gun away now, can't you?" Candlelight pirouetted eerily off the shiny metal barrel.

"I am not certain."

The American sensed this was not going well. "You can trust me," he said. "I know how to maintain a confidence. Besides, you'd be breaking faith with the company."

"But my friend, as you yourself have observed, you are expendable. I believe it was an American who once said: two can keep a secret only if one of them is dead."

The American couldn't afford to give in to the panic he was feeling. "If I die, they have a lever to use against you. You'd be playing right into the hands of the dictator and his generals, the very people you detest. You're too smart for that, too great a man."

Estaban viewed him thoughtfully for a time. He could see the appeal he'd made to the immense ego was working.

"Follow me," Estaban said finally. They went back into the outer room where the leader gathered his chosen disciples around him. "It pleases me to let the American return to his people," Estaban announced in his native tongue. Then Estaban turned back to him and spoke in English. "You will tell your people that Estaban is a man with a heart. I can be generous and fair." He proceeded to give rapid orders.

Juan led him back to the limousine and again pushed him down on the floor. They handled him roughly but he didn't care. He was on his way back; that was all that mattered. The limousine which had been the instrument of his fear and incarceration would now provide his freedom and deliverance. Ironic and yet just, he mused.

Of course, he was fairly certain the company hadn't expected Estaban to actually let him survive. He knew they'd been funneling money to Estaban almost from the beginning. The confidential report he'd managed to read said so. The military junta in power supposedly knew nothing about it. It was a secret, one that would surprise them. After all, company funds backed them as well. Whichever side won, company interests would be protected—or would they? Fascist, communist, terrorist, what difference did the labels really make? One group seemed as cruel, ruthless and repressive as the next. It was the nature of third world politics, he thought with weary cynicism.

The large black limo hit a hard bump and his thoughts returned to Diego's first words to him. It would be Diego and not himself who was food for the piranhas tonight. He supposed there was some satisfaction and comfort in that.

He was suddenly aware that the car stopped moving. Juan turned and thrust a gun forcefully against his head.

"But Estaban said…"

"Not him," Juan's impatient response was in surprisingly flawless English.

"Then who? The company?"

The driver suddenly turned around, smiling with a toothsome grin. He flicked a light with his thumb as if there were a match in his hand but the American saw none. He was convinced it was a trick of some kind. It had to be, didn't it?

"Juan has seen the error of his ways. His loyalty is to me."

"I thought you were dead!"

"As Estaban did. But he will soon learn of his mistake. No, it is you who will be dead. As I told you, some call me El Diablo. It is a name I have justly earned. I promised you would feel the teeth of the piranha and I always keep my word."

Again the ugly smile. The mouth itself made him think of an open grave.

"This is getting old fast." The American was zero at the bone. His teeth began to chatter.

"You are afraid? You should be. Perhaps I might be persuaded to let you live."

"What would you expect in return?"

"Merely your soul."

Did he even have one, he wondered.

The sound of vehicles thundering along the narrow road behind them caught Diego's attention.

"It's the cavalry," the American said. "They're coming to rescue me." He hoped that was true. "There's a homing device beneath the limo's trunk. They've been tracking us."

"Toss him out," Diego said to Juan as he released the automatic door locks. "Perhaps there will be another time for us," Diego said, turning to the American.

"I sincerely hope not," he said. A chill slithered down his spine, despite the heat.

Dazed, he watched from the ground as El Diablo drove the limousine forward. It resembled a sinister, long, black hearse as it moved through the enshrouding vegetation and then suddenly disappeared into the jungle as if it had never existed at all.

One thing was certain: dealing with the devil was a lot like throwing loaded dice. He had taken the wrong fork in the road when he joined the company. He saw that clearly now.

He made a definite decision to leave his current line of employment, end his old life and begin a new one.

✗

Multiple award-winning author, Jacqueline Seewald, has taught creative, expository and technical writing at Rutgers University as well as high school English. Nineteen of her books of fiction have been published. Her most recent mystery is *Death Promise*. Her short stories, poems, essays, reviews and articles have appeared in hundreds of diverse publications and numerous anthologies. Her writer's blog can be found at: http://jacquelineseewald.blogspot.com

"LEASE WITH OPTION TO BUY"

by Ellen Wight

I thought that nothing could compare to the joy I felt when I signed the paperwork to lease the large Victorian at the edge of town. I was wrong. There was so much more joy in my heart as I set fire to it and watched it burn to the ground two months later.

The "lease with option to buy" advertisement leaped out of the newspaper page and I circled it in red right away. You see, it came at the perfect time. I was losing my lease on my very small apartment because the building was being sold. The rent had been cheap and my small salary at a local art gallery left me with little hope of finding something I could afford. So, I called the real estate office handling the property right away and prayed that I was not too late. The price was right and looking back now, I should have questioned why such a large house was going for such a small rent.

Mr. Pyne was the agent in charge of the property and he sounded as excited as I was when he heard that I was interested in leasing the property.

"You're interested in Ridge House! Such a lovely home and at such a reasonable price too. Everything in the house is worth a fortune! You see, the owner is interested in selling to the right person. But, he is most emphatic that it must be the RIGHT person, so a period of a two-year lease is necessary before you will be considered as a buyer."

That should have given me pause. I had never heard of such a strange arrangement. It almost sounded like it was a trial offer to see if I was good enough to be considered to buy the property. The buy option only existed with a two-year lease.

"Mr. Pyne, let me understand you. I have to live in and rent the house for two years to be considered as a buyer? Forgive me, I have little experience with real estate, but isn't that a little unusual?"

"Well, my dear, I have much experience with real estate and that is not at all an unusual request. The owner has the right to decide if you are what the house needs," he said in an almost offended tone. "After all, everything in it is worth a fortune."

I decided to keep quiet and not argue with the man who could ruin the entire deal for me because I was arguing with him. I needed to settle my living situation in a hurry. So what if I had to be on my best behavior for the next two years? I lived alone with no pets and was a tidy and quiet person. So, I set up a time to see the house and met Mr. Pyne at the location one very stormy afternoon.

The house itself was lovely. It was over 200 years old and had all the original woodwork and fixtures. It was already furnished, which was no problem for me as I had very little furniture of my own. The house itself was built on a large ridge of land overlooking the town. Hence, it was named Ridge House. The artistic side of me was in heaven as I wandered through the many rooms of beautiful sculptures and paintings. The house was three stories, had more bedrooms than I could count and very long hallways.

"Do not be overwhelmed, my dear Miss Price. Many of these rooms you will never have to go into. The basement is not safe because of some rotting timbers, so please refrain from going down there. Beyond that, the owner has only one request. NOTHING must be moved or adjusted in the house. All is as it should be. Touch nothing. The house wouldn't like it." He said this in a strange, emphatic voice.

"What do you mean by that?" I asked quickly.

"Nothing, nothing at all," he said, as he recovered his smile quickly.

"Who is the owner of the house? From whom am I renting?" I asked pointedly.

"The owner is a very private person and wishes to remain anonymous," he answered. "Any questions or concerns should be directed to my office. I have handled the arrangements for the house for many years. There is no question I cannot answer."

A warning bell was going off in my head, but the house was so charming that I would have no desire to move anything anyway. So I signed papers and officially was on my way to becoming a homeowner. One week later found me moving boxes and bags into my new home and I felt excited as could be. This was the largest place I had ever lived, but I had to admit that it was a little off the beaten path and isolated. So what, I thought. Peace and quiet after busy days at the gallery was something that I would look forward to. I had enough of the noise of the city.

Trying to get my bearings in the house was my first order of business. A large, winding staircase occupied the center of the main floor as you walked in Surrounding the staircase were numerous doors that were all closed. I began exploring and found that many were living and sitting rooms all of various sizes and colors. As I opened the final door behind the staircase, my heart fell into my shoes. The room was dark and unlit except for a bright, shining light over a portrait on the

far wall over a fireplace. The light shone in a way that made the figures in the picture look like they were not part of a picture. It appeared
that they were standing up. It was an optical illusion, of course, and
took me by surprise, but that is not what spooked me. It was the figures themselves. A man and a woman stood side-by-side staring out
at the viewer. They were dressed in dark period clothing, but the eyes
took my breath away. They were dead, flat looking eyes. They were
like the flat eyes of a doll with no expression or depth. Who would
paint figures with expressionless eyes that looked like they contained
no life? It shocked me so much that I slammed the door and moved
onto the kitchen to continue to unpack. I shook it off with the idea that
I was always too critical when it came to art.

As I continued my work, I began to think that it was odd to keep
the light above the portrait lit. I knew for a fact that no one had lived
in the house for over six months. Why would the real estate agency
keep the light lit? Was it a forgotten light during a showing? The
portrait was gruesome in my opinion and no matter what Mr. Pyne
said, it was going to be taken down. I could not sit in that library with
those dead eyes looking at me. I've seen good and bad art in my years
at the gallery, but those eyes in the portrait were unnerving.

The next morning I marched into the library, switched off the portrait light and took the painting down. I carefully leaned it against the
fireplace and immediately felt better. I had no idea who the people
were in the portrait, and the frame was magnificent. I didn't care. I
hated it. As the weeks went on, I found myself moving other things
as well. I felt guilty because Mr. Pyne had specifically told me not to
touch or move anything, but I rationalized that I was living here now
and the owner had no right to make such demands when I was paying
rent. Moving a small chair here or there certainly would make no difference to anyone, and how would anyone find out in the first place?

The occurrences I noticed were small at first. I would find a chair
moved back to the original place when I know I moved it a few feet
away. A piece of porcelain that I moved closer to the light was back
in its original place. A piece of china was moved a few inches from
where I placed it. I would change things at night, and in the morning
they were back to their original places. But what was most disturbing of all was the portrait. It was hung over the fireplace again with
the portrait light turned on. I knew I wasn't crazy and maybe could
explain everything away except for the portrait. Who was coming in
at night and righting the house? Certainly Mr. Pyne wasn't coming in
in the middle of the night. Certainly no one was breaking in to move
furniture back to its original place. What was going on?

I remembered that he said there was no question about the house he could not answer. I called and while he was not available, I was able to speak to another clerk.

"Mr. Pyne is the sole individual who deals with Ridge House. You should direct all your questions to him."

"I understand that," I said impatiently, "but does anyone else have a key to the house? I think someone else is getting into the house, perhaps at night."

"Miss Price, every house has its own personality, especially Ridge House. Perhaps you made a mistake choosing such a large property. My suggestion is to leave things as you found them. Obviously, the house is not pleased with your changes."

"Are you suggesting the house is alive? How preposterous! Someone is getting into the place at night and making changes. Please have Mr. Pyne call me as soon as possible." And with that, I slammed the phone down.

Mr. Pyne called me later that day and his calm, patronizing voice irritated me.

"Are you having difficulties adjusting, my poor dear?" he crooned.

"No," I snapped. "I'm having difficulty with the idea that someone else is getting into my house and moving things around."

"Miss Price, I told you expressly that nothing was to be touched in the house. All is as it should be. The house does not like changes."

At that, I lost my patience.

"Mr. Pyne, I don't care what the house wants. I want YOU to come and change all the locks to keep out whoever is getting in."

"As you wish," he answered curtly, "but changed locks will not change Ridge House."

After the locks were all changed, the activity seemed to increase. I took the portrait down again and shut it in a closet on the 2nd floor. I began leaving all the lights on in the house, even during the day. I started moving small objects purposely to see if they were changed back to the original positions. They always were. What sent me almost over the edge, though, was one shocking experience.

One particular evening after a long gallery event, all I wanted was to take a long, hot bath and get a good night's sleep. I was not prepared for what waited for me in the bedroom. The portrait that I had shut in the closet on the 2nd floor, now hung over my bed. I was so taken aback and shocked that I bolted from the room, grabbed my phone and called the police. I was crying about an intruder in my house and that I needed immediate help. Of course, after a complete search of the house, nothing was found. When I started to tell my tale of moving objects, I saw the officers look at each other and suggest that I spend the night somewhere else, or at least have someone stay with me that night.

The next day, I decided that I needed answers if I were to stay in the house. It had been a little over two months and I felt like I was losing my mind. I decided to visit the local historical society to see if I could find out any information on the history of the house because I refused to deal with Mr. Pyne's judgmental attitude. The elderly woman at the historical society was very friendly and helpful until she found out that I wanted information on Ridge House.

"Please help me," I implored. I don't think I can last there much longer if I don't get some answers."

The shocking truth was that Ridge House belonged to a man named Jeremiah Pike who built the house with his wife in the early 19th century. It was said that they had a son, although no one was sure, and they kept much to themselves. There were rumors when staff began to disappear seemingly overnight. No one worked for long at Ridge House and it was said that was because Mrs. Pike dabbled in the occult and spirit world and bewitched anyone who worked there. No one ever saw the son and rumors spread that he too had disappeared. Eventually, Mrs. Pike died suddenly and Jeremiah was left in the house alone. He was obsessed with keeping everything as his wife had left it and therefore any remaining staff was forbidden to move any of the furnishings ever. He was seen pacing day and night throughout the large house looking for things that had been moved even an inch while cleaning. His punishments were terrible. He, too, eventually died by hanging himself on the 2nd floor and the house was left to an heir that no one knew.

"How can that be? The house has an owner. Who is it?"

The elderly lady looked sternly at me.

"Ridge House owns itself. My suggestion to you is to get yourself out of there before you become part of its history, too." With that, she turned and left me staring after her with my mouth open.

I had no choice but to go speak with Mr. Pyne again. No one was giving me any answers that would help me figure out what was going on. By the time I got home from the historical society, it was dark and starting to storm. As I entered, the lights refused to go on and I realized that I never asked where the fuse box was. Was it outside? Was it in the locked basement? I lit the candelabra in the front room for light. As I climbed the stairs to the second floor, searching in my bag for my cell phone, a movement caught my eye at the end of the hallway. I looked up and saw a figure of a man standing there, not moving, but staring at me.

"Mr. Pyne? I was just going to call you. Hey, how did you get in here?"

At that point, a flash of lightening from the window lit up the figure at the end of the hallway. It was not Mr. Pyne. It was a man dressed in black period clothes with the dead eyes of a doll just staring. It was the man from the portrait. It was Jeremiah Pike.

I don't remember much after that. I was rooted to the spot in shock, but the sudden movement of the figure at the end of the hall jolted me into action. He began to walk down the hallway headed for me. I bolted down the stairs screaming and crying at the same time. At the end of the stairs, I almost fainted when I collided into yet another figure. It was Mr. Pyne.

"You silly, stupid girl! I told you to leave things along. Now you've angered the house. All is as it must be. Don't you understand?"

I pushed him against the wall and ran for all I was worth screaming and racing for the front door.

"Now you must stay and face the consequences," Mr. Pyne hissed.

"NO!!" I screeched as I fought against him and was aware of the figure in the black period clothing slowly coming down the stairs for me.

As I broke free, I started crashing into everything in the dark. I upset the candelabra that I had lit and it fell crashing against the brocade curtains as I flew through the open door. I saw through the corner of my eye that the curtains were on fire, but all I wanted was to get away from the maniacs inside, both the living one and the dead one. I ran screaming down the street and collided with a policeman who saw the flames on the first floor and was coming to investigate.

The house went up like a torch. I babbled to the police that there was a man inside, but the intensity of the fire prevented anyone from entering. The 200-year old timbers burned quickly and forever. Ridge House was burning to the ground and I was glad.

It wasn't for some time until I got the entire story. The police were able to identify the remains of Mr. Pyne and it was discovered that he was the heir to the Pike property and he was the mysterious owner. No one knew his exact connection to the Pikes, but in order to keep the house, he would rent it for a while and then allow the house to scare any potential buyers away. You see, he never wanted the property to be sold, only paid for. He was the one who must have been coming into the house to rearrange my changes, or did he leave Jeremiah to do that for him? I'll never know.

I received a call from the rental office a few weeks after the fire. The investigation was complete, and faulty wiring was blamed for the fire. I know that I knocked the candelabra over. I watch the curtains catch. But still, the fire department insisted the fire stared on the 2nd floor. I was too tired to argue.

"Miss Price, you were the last occupant of the house and we know that your possessions were lost in the fire. We feel that it is only fair that you are offered the sale of the land since you were the last to occupy the house. No remaining heirs to the property exist."

I told the office emphatically that I was not interested in any land that Ridge House stood on…not now, not ever.

"Well, as you wish," the owner of the agency said, "but we do feel that maybe you would appreciate a token of the house as a remembrance of your time there. In fact, while very little survived the fire, one piece of artwork did. Surely, you appreciate fine art. Would you be interested in the large portrait of the man and woman that used to hang over the fireplace? It is in remarkably good condition, and after all, it must be worth a fortune!"

Ellen Wight has been previously published in Sherlock Holmes Mystery Magazine and currently lives and works in New Hampshire. She gets most of her inspiration from her wonderful family including her husband, 3 children, 6 pets and a horse named Scout. She currently works as a reading specialist in an elementary school, and hopes to inspire others to love reading as much as she does.

THE ADVENTURE OF SILVER BLAZE

by Sir Arthur Conan Doyle

"I am afraid, Watson, that I shall have to go," said Holmes, as we sat down together to our breakfast one morning.

"Go! Where to?"

"To Dartmoor; to King's Pyland."

I was not surprised. Indeed, my only wonder was that he had not already been mixed up in this extraordinary case, which was the one topic of conversation through the length and breadth of England. For a whole day my companion had rambled about the room with his chin upon his chest and his brows knitted, charging and recharging his pipe with the strongest black tobacco, and absolutely deaf to any of my questions or remarks. Fresh editions of every paper had been sent up by our news agent, only to be glanced over and tossed down into a corner. Yet, silent as he was, I knew perfectly well what it was over which he was brooding. There was but one problem before the public which could challenge his powers of analysis, and that was the singular disappearance of the favourite for the Wessex Cup, and the tragic murder of its trainer. When, therefore, he suddenly announced his intention of setting out for the scene of the drama it was only what I had both expected and hoped for.

"I should be most happy to go down with you if I should not be in the way," said I.

"My dear Watson, you would confer a great favour upon me by coming. And I think that your time will not be misspent, for there are points about the case which promise to make it an absolutely unique one. We have, I think, just time to catch our train at Paddington, and I will go further into the matter upon our journey. You would oblige me by bringing with you your very excellent field-glass."

And so it happened that an hour or so later I found myself in the corner of a first-class carriage flying along en route for Exeter, while Sherlock Holmes, with his sharp, eager face framed in his ear-flapped travelling-cap, dipped rapidly into the bundle of fresh papers which he had procured at Paddington. We had left Reading far behind us before he thrust the last one of them under the seat, and offered me his cigar-case.

"We are going well," said he, looking out the window and glancing at his watch. "Our rate at present is fifty-three and a half miles an hour."

"I have not observed the quarter-mile posts," said I.

"Nor have I. But the telegraph posts upon this line are sixty yards apart, and the calculation is a simple one. I presume that you have looked into this matter of the murder of John Straker and the disappearance of Silver Blaze?"

"I have seen what the Telegraph and the Chronicle have to say."

"It is one of those cases where the art of the reasoner should be used rather for the sifting of details than for the acquiring of fresh evidence. The tragedy has been so uncommon, so complete and of such personal importance to so many people, that we are suffering from a plethora of surmise, conjecture, and hypothesis. The difficulty is to detach the framework of fact—of absolute undeniable fact—from the embellishments of theorists and reporters. Then, having established ourselves upon this sound basis, it is our duty to see what inferences may be drawn and what are the special points upon which the whole mystery turns. On Tuesday evening I received telegrams from both Colonel Ross, the owner of the horse, and from Inspector Gregory, who is looking after the case, inviting my co-operation."

"Tuesday evening!" I exclaimed. "And this is Thursday morning. Why didn't you go down yesterday?"

"Because I made a blunder, my dear Watson—which is, I am afraid, a more common occurrence than any one would think who only knew me through your memoirs. The fact is that I could not believe it possible that the most remarkable horse in England could long remain concealed, especially in so sparsely inhabited a place as the north of Dartmoor. From hour to hour yesterday I expected to hear that he had been found, and that his abductor was the murderer of John Straker. When, however, another morning had come, and I found that beyond the arrest of young Fitzroy Simpson nothing had been done, I felt that it was time for me to take action. Yet in some ways I feel that yesterday has not been wasted."

"You have formed a theory, then?"

"At least I have got a grip of the essential facts of the case. I shall enumerate them to you, for nothing clears up a case so much as stating it to another person, and I can hardly expect your co-operation if I do not show you the position from which we start."

I lay back against the cushions, puffing at my cigar, while Holmes, leaning forward, with his long, thin forefinger checking off the points upon the palm of his left hand, gave me a sketch of the events which had led to our journey.

"Silver Blaze," said he, "is from the Isonomy stock, and holds as brilliant a record as his famous ancestor. He is now in his fifth year, and has brought in turn each of the prizes of the turf to Colonel Ross, his fortunate owner. Up to the time of the catastrophe he was the first favorite for the Wessex Cup, the betting being three to one on him. He has always, however, been a prime favourite with the racing public, and has never yet disappointed them, so that even at those odds enormous sums of money have been laid upon him. It is obvious, therefore, that there were many people who had the strongest interest in preventing Silver Blaze from being there at the fall of the flag next Tuesday.

"The fact was, of course, appreciated at King's Pyland, where the Colonel's training-stable is situated. Every precaution was taken to guard the favourite. The trainer, John Straker, is a retired jockey who rode in Colonel Ross's colours before he became too heavy for the weighing-chair. He has served the Colonel for five years as jockey and for seven as trainer, and has always shown himself to be a zealous and honest servant. Under him were three lads; for the establishment was a small one, containing only four horses in all. One of these lads sat up each night in the stable, while the others slept in the loft. All three bore excellent characters. John Straker, who is a married man, lived in a small villa about two hundred yards from the stables. He has no children, keeps one maid-servant, and is comfortably off. The country round is very lonely, but about half a mile to the north there is a small cluster of villas which have been built by a Tavistock contractor for the use of invalids and others who may wish to enjoy the pure Dartmoor air. Tavistock itself lies two miles to the west, while across the moor, also about two miles distant, is the larger training establishment of Mapleton, which belongs to Lord Backwater, and is managed by Silas Brown. In every other direction the moor is a complete wilderness, inhabited only by a few roaming gypsies. Such was the general situation last Monday night when the catastrophe occurred.

"On that evening the horses had been exercised and watered as usual, and the stables were locked up at nine o'clock. Two of the lads walked up to the trainer's house, where they had supper in the kitchen, while the third, Ned Hunter, remained on guard. At a few minutes after nine the maid, Edith Baxter, carried down to the stables his supper, which consisted of a dish of curried mutton. She took no liquid, as there was a water-tap in the stables, and it was the rule that the lad on duty should drink nothing else. The maid carried a lantern with her, as it was very dark and the path ran across the open moor.

"Edith Baxter was within thirty yards of the stables, when a man appeared out of the darkness and called to her to stop. As he stepped into the circle of yellow light thrown by the lantern she saw that he was a person of gentlemanly bearing, dressed in a grey suit of tweeds, with a cloth cap. He wore gaiters, and carried a heavy stick with a knob to it. She was most impressed, however, by the extreme pallor of his face and by the nervousness of his manner. His age, she thought, would be rather over thirty than under it.

"'Can you tell me where I am?' he asked. 'I had almost made up my mind to sleep on the moor, when I saw the light of your lantern.'

"'You are close to the King's Pyland training-stables,' said she.

"'Oh, indeed! What a stroke of luck!' he cried. 'I understand that a stable-boy sleeps there alone every night. Perhaps that is his supper which you are carrying to him. Now I am sure that you would not be too proud to earn the price of a new dress, would you?' He took a piece of white paper folded up out of his waistcoat pocket. 'See that the boy has this to-night, and you shall have the prettiest frock that money can buy.'

"She was frightened by the earnestness of his manner, and ran past him to the window through which she was accustomed to hand the meals. It was already opened, and Hunter was seated at the small table inside. She had begun to tell him of what had happened, when the stranger came up again.

"'Good-evening,' said he, looking through the window. 'I wanted to have a word with you.' The girl has sworn that as he spoke she noticed the corner of the little paper packet protruding from his closed hand.

"'What business have you here?' asked the lad.

"'It's business that may put something into your pocket,' said the other. 'You've two horses in for the Wessex Cup—Silver Blaze and Bayard. Let me have the straight tip and you won't be a loser. Is it a fact that at the weights Bayard could give the other a hundred yards in five furlongs, and that the stable have put their money on him?'

"'So, you're one of those damned touts!' cried the lad. 'I'll show you how we serve them in King's Pyland.' He sprang up and rushed across the stable to unloose the dog. The girl fled away to the house, but as she ran she looked back and saw that the stranger was leaning through the window. A minute later, however, when Hunter rushed out with the hound he was gone, and though he ran all round the buildings he failed to find any trace of him."

"One moment," I asked. "Did the stable-boy, when he ran out with the dog, leave the door unlocked behind him?"

"Excellent, Watson, excellent!" murmured my companion. "The importance of the point struck me so forcibly that I sent a special wire to Dartmoor yesterday to clear the matter up. The boy locked the door before he left it. The window, I may add, was not large enough for a man to get through.

"Hunter waited until his fellow-grooms had returned, when he sent a message to the trainer and told him what had occurred. Straker was excited at hearing the account, although he does not seem to have quite realised its true significance. It left him, however, vaguely uneasy, and Mrs Straker, waking at one in the morning, found that he was dressing. In reply to her inquiries, he said that he could not sleep on account of his anxiety about the horses, and that he intended to walk down to the stables to see that all was well. She begged him to remain at home, as she could hear the rain pattering against the window, but in spite of her entreaties he pulled on his large mackintosh and left the house.

"Mrs Straker awoke at seven in the morning, to find that her husband had not yet returned. She dressed herself hastily, called the maid, and set off for the stables. The door was open; inside, huddled together upon a chair, Hunter was sunk in a state of absolute stupor, the favourite's stall was empty, and there were no signs of his trainer.

"The two lads who slept in the chaff-cutting loft above the harness-room were quickly aroused. They had heard nothing during the night, for they are both sound sleepers. Hunter was obviously under the influence of some powerful drug, and as no sense could be got out of him, he was left to sleep it off while the two lads and the two women ran out in search of the absentees. They still had hopes that the trainer had for some reason taken out the horse for early exercise, but on ascending the knoll near the house, from which all the neighbouring moors were visible, they not only could see no signs of the missing favourite, but they perceived something which warned them that they were in the presence of a tragedy.

"About a quarter of a mile from the stables John Straker's overcoat was flapping from a furze-bush. Immediately beyond there was a bowl-shaped depression in the moor, and at the bottom of this was found the dead body of the unfortunate trainer. His head had been shattered by a savage blow from some heavy weapon, and he was wounded on the thigh, where there was a long, clean cut, inflicted evidently by some very sharp instrument. It was clear, however, that Straker had defended himself vigorously against his assailants, for in his right hand he held a small knife, which was clotted with blood up to the handle, while in his left he clasped a red and black silk cravat, which was recognised by the maid as having been worn on the preceding evening by the stranger who had visited the stables. Hunter, on recovering from his stupor, was also quite positive as to the ownership of the cravat. He was equally certain that the same stranger had, while standing at the window, drugged his curried mutton, and so deprived the stables of their watchman. As to the missing horse, there were abundant proofs in the mud which lay at the bottom of the fatal hollow that he had been there at the time of the struggle. But from that morning he has disappeared, and although a large reward has been offered, and all the gypsies of Dartmoor are on the alert, no news has come of him. Finally, an analysis has shown that the remains of his supper left by the stable-lad contain an appreciable quantity of powdered opium, while the people at the house partook of the same dish on the same night without any ill effect.

"Those are the main facts of the case, stripped of all surmise, and stated as baldly as possible. I shall now recapitulate what the police have done in the matter.

"Inspector Gregory, to whom the case has been committed, is an extremely competent officer. Were he but gifted with imagination he might rise to great heights in his profession. On his arrival he promptly found and arrested the man upon whom suspicion naturally rested. There was little difficulty in finding him, for he inhabited one of those villas which I have mentioned. His name, it appears, was Fitzroy Simpson. He was a man of excellent birth and education, who had squandered a fortune upon the turf, and who lived now by doing a little quiet and genteel book-making in the sporting clubs of London. An examination of his betting-book shows that bets to the amount of five thousand pounds had been registered by him against the favourite. On being arrested he volunteered that statement that he had come down to Dartmoor in the hope of getting some information about the King's Pyland horses, and also about Desborough, the second favourite, which was in charge of Silas Brown at the Mapleton stables. He did not attempt to deny that he had acted as described upon the evening before, but declared that he had no sinister designs, and had simply wished to obtain first-hand information. When confronted with his cravat, he turned very pale, and was utterly unable to account for its presence in the hand of the murdered man. His wet clothing showed that he had been out in the storm of the night before, and his stick, which was a Penang-lawyer weighted with lead, was just such a weapon as might, by repeated blows, have inflicted the terrible injuries to which the trainer had succumbed. On the other hand, there was no wound upon his person, while the state of Straker's knife would show that one at least of his assailants must bear his mark upon him. There you have it all in a nutshell, Watson, and if you can give me any light I shall be infinitely obliged to you."

I had listened with the greatest interest to the statement which Holmes, with characteristic clearness, had laid before me. Though most of the facts were familiar to me, I had not sufficiently appreci-ated their relative importance, nor their connection to each other.

"Is it not possible," I suggested, "that the incised wound upon Straker may have been caused by his own knife in the convulsive struggles which follow any brain injury?"

"It is more than possible; it is probable," said Holmes. "In that case one of the main points in favour of the accused disappears."

"And yet," said I, "even now I fail to understand what the theory of the police can be."

"I am afraid that whatever theory we state has very grave objec-tions to it," returned my companion. "The police imagine, I take it, that this Fitzroy Simpson, having drugged the lad, and having in some way obtained a duplicate key, opened the stable door and took out the horse, with the intention, apparently, of kidnapping him altogether. His bridle is missing, so that Simpson must have put this on. Then, having left the door open behind him, he was leading the horse away over the moor, when he was either met or overtaken by the trainer. A row naturally ensued. Simpson beat out the trainer's brains with his heavy stick without receiving any injury from the small knife which Straker used in self-defence, and then the thief either led the horse on to some secret hiding-place, or else it may have bolted during the struggle, and be now wandering out on the moors. That is the case as it appears to the police, and improbable as it is, all other explanations are more improbable still. However, I shall very quickly test the mat-ter when I am once upon the spot, and until then I cannot really see how we can get much further than our present position."

It was evening before we reached the little town of Tavistock, which lies, like the boss of a shield, in the middle of the huge circle of Dartmoor. Two gentlemen were awaiting us in the station—the one a tall, fair man with lion-like hair and beard and curiously penetrating light blue eyes; the other a small, alert person, very neat and dapper, in a frock-coat and gaiters, with trim little side-whiskers and an eye-glass. The latter was Colonel Ross, the well-known sportsman; the other, Inspector Gregory, a man who was rapidly making his name in the English detective service.

"I am delighted that you have come down, Mr Holmes," said the Colonel. "The Inspector here has done all that could possibly be sug-gested, but I wish to leave no stone unturned in trying to avenge poor Straker and in recovering my horse."

"Have there been any fresh developments?" asked Holmes.

"I am sorry to say that we have made very little progress," said the Inspector. "We have an open carriage outside, and as you would no doubt like to see the place before the light fails, we might talk it over as we drive."

A minute later we were all seated in a comfortable landau, and were rattling through the quaint old Devonshire city. Inspector Gregory was full of his case, and poured out a stream of remarks, while Holmes threw in an occasional question or interjection. Colonel Ross leaned back with his arms folded and his hat tilted over his eyes, while I listened with interest to the dialogue of the two detectives. Gregory was formulating his theory, which was almost exactly what Holmes had foretold in the train.

"The net is drawn pretty close round Fitzroy Simpson," he remarked, "and I believe myself that he is our man. At the same time I recognise that the evidence is purely circumstantial, and that some new development may upset it."

"How about Straker's knife?"

"We have quite come to the conclusion that he wounded himself in his fall."

"My friend Dr Watson made that suggestion to me as we came down. If so, it would tell against this man Simpson."

"Undoubtedly. He has neither a knife nor any sign of a wound. The evidence against him is certainly very strong. He had a great interest in the disappearance of the favourite. He lies under suspicion of having poisoned the stable-boy, he was undoubtedly out in the storm, he was armed with a heavy stick, and his cravat was found in the dead man's hand. I really think we have enough to go before a jury."

Holmes shook his head. "A clever counsel would tear it all to rags," said he. "Why should he take the horse out of the stable? If he wished to injure it why could he not do it there? Has a duplicate key been found in his possession? What chemist sold him the powdered opium? Above all, where could he, a stranger to the district, hide a horse, and such a horse as this? What is his own explanation as to the paper which he wished the maid to give to the stable-boy?"

"He says that it was a ten-pound note. One was found in his purse. But your other difficulties are not so formidable as they seem. He is not a stranger to the district. He has twice lodged at Tavistock in the summer. The opium was probably brought from London. The key, having served its purpose, would be hurled away. The horse may be at the bottom of one of the pits or old mines upon the moor."

"What does he say about the cravat?"

"He acknowledges that it is his, and declares that he had lost it. But a new element has been introduced into the case which may account for his leading the horse from the stable."

Holmes pricked up his ears.

"We have found traces which show that a party of gypsies en-camped on Monday night within a mile of the spot where the murder took place. On Tuesday they were gone. Now, presuming that there was some understanding between Simpson and these gypsies, might he not have been leading the horse to them when he was overtaken, and may they not have him now?"

"It is certainly possible."

"The moor is being scoured for these gypsies. I have also examined every stable and out-house in Tavistock, and for a radius of ten miles."

"There is another training-stable quite close, I understand?"

"Yes, and that is a factor which we must certainly not neglect. As Desborough, their horse, was second in the betting, they had an interest in the disappearance of the favourite. Silas Brown, the trainer, is known to have had large bets upon the event, and he was no friend to poor Straker. We have, however, examined the stables, and there is nothing to connect him with the affair."

"And nothing to connect this man Simpson with the interests of the Mapleton stables?"

"Nothing at all."

Holmes leaned back in the carriage, and the conversation ceased. A few minutes later our driver pulled up at a neat little red-brick villa with overhanging eaves which stood by the road. Some distance off, across a paddock, lay a long grey-tiled out-building. In every other direction the low curves of the moor, bronze-coloured from the fading ferns, stretched away to the sky-line, broken only by the steeples of Tavistock, and by a cluster of houses away to the westward which marked the Mapleton stables. We all sprang out with the exception of Holmes, who continued to lean back with his eyes fixed upon the sky in front of him, entirely absorbed in his own thoughts. It was only when I touched his arm that he roused himself with a violent start and stepped out of the carriage.

"Excuse me," said he, turning to Colonel Ross, who had looked at him in some surprise. "I was day-dreaming." There was a gleam in his eyes and a suppressed excitement in his manner which convinced me, used as I was to his ways, that his hand was upon a clue, though I could not imagine where he had found it.

"Perhaps you would prefer at once to go on to the scene of the crime, Mr Holmes?" said Gregory.

"I think that I should prefer to stay here a little and go into one or two questions of detail. Straker was brought back here, I presume?"

"Yes; he lies upstairs. The inquest is to-morrow."

"He has been in your service some years, Colonel Ross?"

"I have always found him an excellent servant."

"I presume that you made an inventory of what he had in his pockets at the time of his death, Inspector?"

"I have the things themselves in the sitting-room, if you would care to see them."

"I should be very glad."

We all filed into the front room and sat round the central table while the Inspector unlocked a square tin box and laid a small heap of things before us. There was a box of vestas, two inches of tallow candle, an A.D.P. brier-root pipe, a pouch of seal-skin with half an ounce of long-cut Cavendish, a silver watch with a gold chain, five sovereigns in gold, an aluminium pencil-case, a few papers, and an ivory-handled knife with a very delicate, inflexible blade marked Weiss & Co., London.

"This is a very singular knife," said Holmes, lifting it up and examining it minutely. "I presume, as I see blood-stains upon it, that it is the one which was found in the dead man's grasp. Watson, this knife is surely in your line?"

"It is what we call a cataract knife," said I.

"I thought so. A very delicate blade devised for very delicate work. A strange thing for a man to carry with him upon a rough expedition, especially as it would not shut in his pocket."

"The tip was guarded by a disk of cork which we found beside his body," said the Inspector. "His wife tells us that the knife had lain upon the dressing-table, and that he had picked it up as he left the room. It was a poor weapon, but perhaps the best that he could lay his hands on at the moment."

"Very possible. How about these papers?"

"Three of them are receipted hay-dealers' accounts. One of them is a letter of instructions from Colonel Ross. This other is a milliner's account for thirty-seven pounds fifteen made out by Madame Lesurier, of Bond Street, to William Derbyshire. Mrs Straker tells us that Derbyshire was a friend of her husband's and that occasionally his letters were addressed here."

"Madam Derbyshire had somewhat expensive tastes," remarked Holmes, glancing down the account. "Twenty-two guineas is rather heavy for a single costume. However there appears to be nothing more to learn, and we may now go down to the scene of the crime."

As we emerged from the sitting-room a woman, who had been waiting in the passage, took a step forward and laid her hand upon the Inspector's sleeve. Her face was haggard and thin and eager, stamped with the print of a recent horror.

"Have you got them? Have you found them?" she panted.

"No, Mrs Straker. But Mr Holmes here has come from London to help us, and we shall do all that is possible."

"Surely I met you in Plymouth at a garden-party some little time ago, Mrs Straker?" said Holmes.

"No, sir; you are mistaken."

"Dear me! Why, I could have sworn to it. You wore a costume of dove-coloured silk with ostrich-feather trimming."

"I never had such a dress, sir," answered the lady.

"Ah, that quite settles it," said Holmes. And with an apology he followed the Inspector outside. A short walk across the moor took us to the hollow in which the body had been found. At the brink of it was the furze-bush upon which the coat had been hung.

"There was no wind that night, I understand," said Holmes.

"None; but very heavy rain."

"In that case the overcoat was not blown against the furze-bush, but placed there."

"Yes, it was laid across the bush."

"You fill me with interest, I perceive that the ground has been trampled up a good deal. No doubt many feet have been here since Monday night."

"A piece of matting has been laid here at the side, and we have all stood upon that."

"Excellent."

"In this bag I have one of the boots which Straker wore, one of Fitzroy Simpson's shoes, and a cast horseshoe of Silver Blaze."

"My dear Inspector, you surpass yourself!" Homes took the bag, and, descending into the hollow, he pushed the matting into a more central position. Then stretching himself upon his face and leaning his chin upon his hands, he made a careful study of the trampled mud in front of him. "Hullo!" said he, suddenly. "What's this?" It was a wax vesta half burned, which was so coated with mud that it looked at first like a little chip of wood.

"I cannot think how I came to overlook it," said the Inspector, with an expression of annoyance.

"It was invisible, buried in the mud. I only saw it because I was looking for it."

"What! You expected to find it?"

"I thought it not unlikely."

He took the boots from the bag, and compared the impressions of each of them with marks upon the ground. Then he clambered up to the rim of the hollow, and crawled about among the ferns and bushes.

"I am afraid that there are no more tracks," said the Inspector. "I have examined the ground very carefully for a hundred yards in each direction."

"Indeed!" said Holmes, rising. "I should not have the impertinence to do it again after what you say. But I should like to take a little walk over the moor before it grows dark, that I may know my ground to-morrow, and I think that I shall put this horseshoe into my pocket for luck."

Colonel Ross, who had shown some signs of impatience at my companion's quiet and systematic method of work, glanced at his watch. "I wish you would come back with me, Inspector," said he. "There are several points on which I should like your advice, and especially as to whether we do not owe it to the public to remove our horse's name from the entries for the Cup."

"Certainly not," cried Holmes, with decision. "I should let the name stand."

The Colonel bowed. "I am very glad to have had your opinion, sir," said he. "You will find us at poor Straker's house when you have finished your walk, and we can drive together into Tavistock."

He turned back with the Inspector, while Holmes and I walked slowly across the moor. The sun was beginning to sink behind the stables of Mapleton, and the long, sloping plain in front of us was tinged with gold, deepening into rich, ruddy browns where the faded ferns and brambles caught the evening light. But the glories of the landscape were all wasted upon my companion, who was sunk in the deepest thought.

"It's this way, Watson," said he at last. "We may leave the question of who killed John Straker for the instant, and confine ourselves to finding out what has become of the horse. Now, supposing that he broke away during or after the tragedy, where could he have gone to? The horse is a very gregarious creature. If left to himself his instincts would have been either to return to King's Pyland or go over to Mapleton. Why should he run wild upon the moor? He would surely have been seen by now. And why should gypsies kidnap him? These people always clear out when they hear of trouble, for they do not wish to be pestered by the police. They could not hope to sell such a horse. They would run a great risk and gain nothing by taking him. Surely that is clear."

"Where is he, then?"

"I have already said that he must have gone to King's Pyland or to Mapleton. He is not at King's Pyland. Therefore he is at Mapleton. Let us take that as a working hypothesis and see what it leads us to. This part of the moor, as the Inspector remarked, is very hard and dry.

But if falls away towards Mapleton, and you can see from here that there is a long hollow over yonder, which must have been very wet on Monday night. If our supposition is correct, then the horse must have crossed that, and there is the point where we should look for his tracks."

We had been walking briskly during this conversation, and a few more minutes brought us to the hollow in question. At Holmes's request I walked down the bank to the right, and he to the left, but I had not taken fifty paces before I heard him give a shout, and saw him waving his hand to me. The track of a horse was plainly outlined in the soft earth in front of him, and the shoe which he took from his pocket exactly fitted the impression.

"See the value of imagination," said Holmes. "It is the one quality which Gregory lacks. We imagined what might have happened, acted upon the supposition, and find ourselves justified. Let us proceed."

We crossed the marshy bottom and passed over a quarter of a mile of dry, hard turf. Again the ground sloped, and again we came on the tracks. Then we lost them for half a mile, but only to pick them up once more quite close to Mapleton. It was Holmes who saw them first, and he stood pointing with a look of triumph upon his face. A man's track was visible beside the horse's.

"The horse was alone before," I cried.

"Quite so. It was alone before. Hullo, what is this?"

The double track turned sharp off and took the direction of King's Pyland. Homes whistled, and we both followed along after it. His eyes were on the trail, but I happened to look a little to one side, and saw to my surprise the same tracks coming back again in the opposite direction.

"One for you, Watson," said Holmes, when I pointed it out. "You have saved us a long walk, which would have brought us back on our own traces. Let us follow the return track."

We had not to go far. It ended at the paving of asphalt which led up to the gates of the Mapleton stables. As we approached, a groom ran out from them.

"We don't want any loiterers about here," said he.

"I only wished to ask a question," said Holmes, with his finger and thumb in his waistcoat pocket. "Should I be too early to see your master, Mr Silas Brown, if I were to call at five o'clock to-morrow morning?"

"Bless you, sir, if any one is about he will be, for he is always the first stirring. But here he is, sir, to answer your questions for himself. No, sir, no; it is as much as my place is worth to let him see me touch your money. Afterwards, if you like."

As Sherlock Holmes replaced the half-crown which he had drawn from his pocket, a fierce-looking elderly man strode out from the gate with a hunting-crop swinging in his hand.

"What's this, Dawson!" he cried. "No gossiping! Go about your business! And you, what the devil do you want here?"

"Ten minutes' talk with you, my good sir," said Holmes in the sweetest of voices.

"I've no time to talk to every gadabout. We want no stranger here. Be off, or you may find a dog at your heels."

Holmes leaned forward and whispered something in the trainer's ear. He started violently and flushed to the temples.

"It's a lie!" he shouted. "An infernal lie!"

"Very good. Shall we argue about it here in public or talk it over in your parlour?"

"Oh, come in if you wish to."

Holmes smiled. "I shall not keep you more than a few minutes, Watson," said he. "Now, Mr Brown, I am quite at your disposal."

It was twenty minutes, and the reds had all faded into greys before Holmes and the trainer reappeared. Never have I seen such a change as had been brought about in Silas Brown in that short time. His face was ashy pale, beads of perspiration shone upon his brow, and his hands shook until the hunting-crop wagged like a branch in the wind. His bullying, overbearing manner was all gone too, and he cringed along at my companion's side like a dog with its master.

"You instructions will be done. It shall all be done," said he.

"There must be no mistake," said Holmes, looking round at him. The other winced as he read the menace in his eyes.

"Oh no, there shall be no mistake. It shall be there. Should I change it first or not?"

Holmes thought a little and then burst out laughing. "No, don't," said he; "I shall write to you about it. No tricks, now, or—"

"Oh, you can trust me, you can trust me!"

"Yes, I think I can. Well, you shall hear from me to-morrow." He turned upon his heel, disregarding the trembling hand which the other held out to him, and we set off for King's Pyland.

"A more perfect compound of the bully, coward, and sneak than Master Silas Brown I have seldom met with," remarked Holmes as we trudged along together.

"He has the horse, then?"

"He tried to bluster out of it, but I described to him so exactly what his actions had been upon that morning that he is convinced that I was watching him. Of course you observed the peculiarly square toes in the impressions, and that his own boots exactly corresponded to them. Again, of course no subordinate would have dared to do such a thing. I described to him how, when according to his custom he was the first down, he perceived a strange horse wandering over the moor. How he went out to it, and his astonishment at recognising, from the white forehead which has given the favourite its name, that chance had put in his power the only horse which could beat the one upon which he had put his money. Then I described how his first impulse had been to lead him back to King's Pyland, and how the devil had shown him how he could hide the horse until the race was over, and how he had led it back and concealed it at Mapleton. When I told him every detail he gave it up and thought only of saving his own skin."

"But his stables had been searched?"

"Oh, an old horse-fakir like him has many a dodge."

"But are you not afraid to leave the horse in his power now, since he has every interest in injuring it?"

"My dear fellow, he will guard it as the apple of his eye. He knows that his only hope of mercy is to produce it safe."

"Colonel Ross did not impress me as a man who would be likely to show much mercy in any case."

"The matter does not rest with Colonel Ross. I follow my own methods, and tell as much or as little as I choose. That is the advantage of being unofficial. I don't know whether you observed it, Watson, but the Colonel's manner has been just a trifle cavalier to me. I am inclined now to have a little amusement at his expense. Say nothing to him about the horse."

"Certainly not without your permission."

"And of course this is all quite a minor point compared to the question of who killed John Straker."

"And you will devote yourself to that?"

"On the contrary, we both go back to London by the night train."

I was thunderstruck by my friend's words. We had only been a few hours in Devonshire, and that he should give up an investigation which he had begun so brilliantly was quite incomprehensible to me. Not a word more could I draw from him until we were back at the trainer's house. The Colonel and the Inspector were awaiting us in the parlour.

"My friend and I return to town by the night-express," said Holmes. "We have had a charming little breath of your beautiful Dartmoor air."

The Inspector opened his eyes, and the Colonel's lip curled in a sneer.

"So you despair of arresting the murderer of poor Straker," said he.

Holmes shrugged his shoulders. "There are certainly grave difficulties in the way," said he. "I have every hope, however, that your horse will start upon Tuesday, and I beg that you will have your jockey in readiness. Might I ask for a photograph of Mr John Straker?"

The Inspector took one from an envelope and handed it to him.

"My dear Gregory, you anticipate all my wants. If I might ask you to wait here for an instant, I have a question which I should like to put to the maid."

"I must say that I am rather disappointed in our London consultant," said Colonel Ross, bluntly, as my friend left the room. "I do not see that we are any further than when he came."

"At least you have his assurance that your horse will run," said I.

"Yes, I have his assurance," said the Colonel, with a shrug of his shoulders. "I should prefer to have the horse."

I was about to make some reply in defence of my friend when he entered the room again.

"Now, gentlemen," said he, "I am quite ready for Tavistock."

As we stepped into the carriage one of the stable-lads held the door open for us. A sudden idea seemed to occur to Holmes, for he leaned forward and touched the lad upon the sleeve.

"You have a few sheep in the paddock," he said. "Who attends to them?"

"I do, sir."

"Have you noticed anything amiss with them of late?"

"Well, sir, not of much account; but three of them have gone lame, sir."

I could see that Holmes was extremely pleased, for he chuckled and rubbed his hands together.

"A long shot, Watson; a very long shot," said he, pinching my arm. "Gregory, let me recommend to your attention this singular epidemic among the sheep. Drive on, coachman!"

Colonel Ross still wore an expression which showed the poor opinion which he had formed of my companion's ability, but I saw by the Inspector's face that his attention had been keenly aroused.

"You consider that to be important?" he asked.

"Exceedingly so."

"Is there any point to which you would wish to draw my attention?"

"To the curious incident of the dog in the night-time."

"The dog did nothing in the night-time."

"That was the curious incident," remarked Sherlock Holmes.

Four days later Holmes and I were again in the train, bound for Winchester to see the race for the Wessex Cup. Colonel Ross met us by appointment outside the station, and we drove in his drag to the course beyond the town. His face was grave, and his manner was cold in the extreme. "I have seen nothing of my horse," said he.

"I suppose that you would know him when you saw him?" asked Holmes.

The Colonel was very angry. "I have been on the turf for twenty years, and never was asked such a question as that before," said he. "A child would know Silver Blaze, with his white forehead and his mottled off-foreleg."

"How is the betting?"

"Well, that is the curious part of it. You could have got fifteen to one yesterday, but the price has become shorter and shorter, until you can hardly get three to one now."

"Hum!" said Holmes. "Somebody knows something, that is clear."

As the drag drew up in the enclosure near the grand stand I glanced at the card to see the entries.

Wessex Plate [it ran] 50 sovs. each h ft with 1000 sovs. added for four- and five-year olds. Second, £300. Third, £200. New course (one mile and five furlongs).

1. Mr Heath Newton's The Negro (red cap, cinnamon jacket).

2. Colonel Wardlaw's Pugilist (pink cap, blue and black jacket).

3. Lord Backwater's Desborough (yellow cap and sleeves).

4. Colonel Ross's Silver Blaze (black cap, red jacket).

5. Duke of Balmoral's Iris (yellow and black stripes).

6. Lord Singleford's Rasper (purple cap, black sleeves).

"We scratched our other one, and put all hopes on your word," said the Colonel. "Why, what is that? Silver Blaze favourite?"

"Five to four against Silver Blaze!" roared the ring. "Five to four against Silver Blaze! Five to fifteen against Desborough! Five to four on the field!"

"There are the numbers up," I cried. "They are all six there."

"All six there? Then my horse is running," cried the Colonel in great agitation. "But I don't see him. My colours have not passed."

"Only five have passed. This must be he."

As I spoke a powerful bay horse swept out from the weighting enclosure and cantered past us, bearing on it back the well-known black and red of the Colonel.

"That's not my horse," cried the owner. "That beast has not a white hair upon its body. What is this that you have done, Mr Holmes?"

"Well, well, let us see how he gets on," said my friend, imperturbably. For a few minutes he gazed through my field-glass. "Capital! An excellent start!" he cried suddenly. "There they are, coming round the curve!"

From our drag we had a superb view as they came up the straight. The six horses were so close together that a carpet could have covered them, but half way up the yellow of the Mapleton stable showed to the front. Before they reached us, however, Desborough's bolt was shot, and the Colonel's horse, coming away with a rush, passed the post a good six lengths before its rival, the Duke of Balmoral's Iris making a bad third.

"It's my race, anyhow," gasped the Colonel, passing his hand over his eyes. "I confess that I can make neither head nor tail of it. Don't you think that you have kept up your mystery long enough, Mr Holmes?"

"Certainly, Colonel, you shall know everything. Let us all go round and have a look at the horse together. Here he is," he continued, as we made our way into the weighing enclosure, where only owners and their friends find admittance. "You have only to wash his face and his leg in spirits of wine, and you will find that he is the same old Silver Blaze as ever."

"You take my breath away!"

"I found him in the hands of a fakir, and took the liberty of running him just as he was sent over."

"My dear sir, you have done wonders. The horse looks very fit and well. It never went better in its life. I owe you a thousand apologies for having doubted your ability. You have done me a great service by recovering my horse. You would do me a greater still if you could lay your hands on the murderer of John Straker."

"I have done so," said Holmes quietly.

The Colonel and I stared at him in amazement. "You have got him! Where is he, then?"

"He is here."

"Here! Where?"

"In my company at the present moment."

The Colonel flushed angrily. "I quite recognise that I am under obligations to you, Mr Holmes," said he, "but I must regard what you have just said as either a very bad joke or an insult."

Sherlock Holmes laughed. "I assure you that I have not associated you with the crime, Colonel," said he. "The real murderer is standing immediately behind you." He stepped past and laid his hand upon the glossy neck of the thoroughbred.

"The horse!" cried both the Colonel and myself.

"Yes, the horse. And it may lessen his guilt if I say that it was done in self-defence, and that John Straker was a man who was entirely unworthy of your confidence. But there goes the bell, and as I stand to win a little on this next race, I shall defer a lengthy explanation until a more fitting time."

We had the corner of a Pullman car to ourselves that evening as we whirled back to London, and I fancy that the journey was a short one to Colonel Ross as well as to myself, as we listened to our companion's narrative of the events which had occurred at the Dartmoor training-stables upon the Monday night, and the means by which he had unravelled them.

"I confess," said he, "that any theories which I had formed from the newspaper reports were entirely erroneous. And yet there were indications there, had they not been overlaid by other details which concealed their true import. I went to Devonshire with the conviction that Fitzroy Simpson was the true culprit, although, of course, I saw that the evidence against him was by no means complete. It was while I was in the carriage, just as we reached the trainer's house, that the immense significance of the curried mutton occurred to me. You may remember that I was distrait, and remained sitting after you had all alighted. I was marvelling in my own mind how I could possibly have overlooked so obvious a clue."

"I confess," said the Colonel, "that even now I cannot see how it helps us."

"It was the first link in my chain of reasoning. Powdered opium is by no means tasteless. The flavour is not disagreeable, but it is perceptible. Were it mixed with any ordinary dish the eater would undoubtedly detect it, and would probably eat no more. A curry was exactly the medium which would disguise this taste. By no possible supposition could this stranger, Fitzroy Simpson, have caused curry to be served in the trainer's family that night, and it is surely too monstrous a coincidence to suppose that he happened to come along with powdered opium upon the very night when a dish happened to be served which would disguise the flavour. That is unthinkable. Therefore Simpson becomes eliminated from the case, and our attention centres upon Straker and his wife, the only two people who could have chosen curried mutton for supper that night. The opium was added after the dish was set aside for the stable-boy, for the others had the same for supper with no ill effects. Which of them, then, had access to that dish without the maid seeing them?

"Before deciding that question I had grasped the significance of the silence of the dog, for one true inference invariably suggests others. The Simpson incident had shown me that a dog was kept in the stables, and yet, though some one had been in and had fetched out a horse, he had not barked enough to arouse the two lads in the loft. Obviously the midnight visitor was some one whom the dog knew well.

"I was already convinced, or almost convinced, that John Straker went down to the stables in the dead of the night and took out Silver Blaze. For what purpose? For a dishonest one, obviously, or why should he drug his own stable-boy? And yet I was at a loss to know why. There have been cases before now where trainers have made sure of great sums of money by laying against their own horses, through agents, and then preventing them from winning by fraud. Sometimes it is a pulling jockey. Sometimes it is some surer and subtler means. What was it here? I hoped that the contents of his pockets might help me to form a conclusion.

"And they did so. You cannot have forgotten the singular knife which was found in the dead man's hand, a knife which certainly no sane man would choose for a weapon. It was, as Dr Watson told us, a form of knife which is used for the most delicate operations known in surgery. And it was to be used for a delicate operation that night. You must know, with your wide experience of turf matters, Colonel Ross, that it is possible to make a slight nick upon the tendons of a horse's ham, and to do it subcutaneously, so as to leave absolutely no trace. A horse so treated would develop a slight lameness, which would be put down to a strain in exercise or a touch of rheumatism, but never to foul play."

"Villain! Scoundrel!" cried the Colonel.

"We have here the explanation of why John Straker wished to take the horse out on to the moor. So spirited a creature would have certainly roused the soundest of sleepers when it felt the prick of the knife. It was absolutely necessary to do it in the open air."

"I have been blind!" cried the Colonel. "Of course that was why he needed the candle, and struck the match."

"Undoubtedly. But in examining his belongings I was fortunate enough to discover not only the method of the crime, but even its motives. As a man of the world, Colonel, you know that men do not carry other people's bills about in their pockets. We have most of us quite enough to do to settle our own. I at once concluded that Straker was leading a double life, and keeping a second establishment. The nature of the bill showed that there was a lady in the case, and one who had expensive tastes. Liberal as you are with your servants, one can hardly expect that they can buy twenty-guinea walking dresses for their ladies. I questioned Mrs Straker as to the dress without her knowing it, and having satisfied myself that it had never reached her, I made a note of the milliner's address, and felt that by calling there with Straker's photograph I could easily dispose of the mythical Derbyshire.

"From that time on all was plain. Straker had led out the horse to a hollow where his light would be invisible. Simpson in his flight had dropped his cravat, and Straker had picked it up—with some idea, perhaps, that he might use it in securing the horse's leg. Once in the hollow, he had got behind the horse and had struck a light; but the creature frightened at the sudden glare, and with the strange instinct of animals feeling that some mischief was intended, had lashed out, and the steel shoe had struck Straker full on the forehead. He had already, in spite of the rain, taken off his overcoat in order to do his delicate task, and so, as he fell, his knife gashed his thigh. Do I make it clear?"

"Wonderful!" cried the Colonel. "Wonderful! You might have been there!"

"My final shot was, I confess a very long one. It struck me that so astute a man as Straker would not undertake this delicate tendon-nicking without a little practice. What could he practice on? My eyes fell upon the sheep, and I asked a question which, rather to my surprise, showed that my surmise was correct.

"When I returned to London I called upon the milliner, who had recognised Straker as an excellent customer of the name of Derbyshire, who had a very dashing wife, with a strong partiality for expensive dresses. I have no doubt that this woman had plunged him over head and ears in debt, and so led him into this miserable plot."

"You have explained all but one thing," cried the Colonel. "Where was the horse?"

"Ah, it bolted, and was cared for by one of your neighbours. We must have an amnesty in that direction, I think. This is Clapham Junction, if I am not mistaken, and we shall be in Victoria in less than ten minutes. If you care to smoke a cigar in our rooms, Colonel, I shall be happy to give you any other details which might interest you."

www.ingramcontent.com/pod-product-compliance
Lightning Source LLC
Chambersburg PA
CBHW050823180626
46814CB00004B/1425